USA TODAY BESTSELLING AUTHOR
# DALE MAYER

# Gun in the Gardenias

Lovely Lethal Gardens 7

GUN IN THE GARDENIAS: LOVELY LETHAL GARDENS,
BOOK 7
Beverly Dale Mayer
Valley Publishing Ltd.

Copyright © 2019



ISBN-13: 978-1-773361-91-8
Print Edition

# Books in This Series:

Arsenic in the Azaleas, Book 1

Bones in the Begonias, Book 2

Corpse in the Carnations, Book 3

Daggers in the Dahlias, Book 4

Evidence in the Echinacea, Book 5

Footprints in the Ferns, Book 6

Gun in the Gardenias, Book 7

Handcuffs in the Heather, Book 8

Ice Pick in the Ivy, Book 9

Jewels in the Juniper, Book 10

Killer in the Kiwis, Book 11

Lifeless in the Lilies, Book 12

Murder in the Marigolds, Book 13

Nabbed in the Nasturtiums, Book 14

Offed in the Orchids, Book 15

Poison in the Pansies, Book 16

Quarry in the Quince, Book 17

Revenge in the Roses, Book 18

Silenced in the Sunflowers, Book 19

Toes in the Tulips, Book 20

Lovely Lethal Gardens, Books 1–2

Lovely Lethal Gardens, Books 3–4

Lovely Lethal Gardens, Books 5–6

Lovely Lethal Gardens, Books 7–8

Lovely Lethal Gardens, Books 9–10

# About This Book

**A new cozy mystery series from USA Today best-selling author Dale Mayer. Follow gardener and amateur sleuth Doreen Montgomery—and her amusing and mostly lovable cat, dog, and parrot—as they catch murderers and solve crimes in lovely Kelowna, British Columbia.**

*Riches to rags. ... Chaos to more chaos. ... Fire destroys evidence. ... Or at least most of it!*

Flush with success from solving a decade-old kidnapping case, Doreen can't wait to find out what's next in her one-woman crusade to clean up Kelowna's cold crimes. But, before she can unearth another old case to sink her teeth into, she must tie up some loose ends from the last one.

Steve Albright, fixer for the local biker gang, has made it clear that he blames Doreen for sending his friend Penny Jordan to prison. Steve even suggests that Doreen might have set up Penny Jordan. While Doreen wouldn't do that, she's afraid that other people might believe Steve. He's a popular figure in town and has a lot of friends, many of whom Doreen doesn't want to get any closer to than she must.

At least Steve doesn't have his gun anymore, having dropped that in Doreen's neighbor's gardenia bed while she chased him from her yard. Which makes Doreen think that maybe it's safe to dig into Steve's past. Until she uncovers a connection to three arson cases from years ago and is warned off by Corporal Mack Moreau.

But Doreen's never listened to Mack before, and it has

all worked out thus far, so it's not like she has to listen to him now. Right?

**Sign up to be notified of all Dale's releases here!**
https://geni.us/DaleNews

# Chapter 1

*Wednesday Dinnertime, … Later the Same Day after Closing Her Last Case*

IT WAS CRAZY to think how quickly this case had solved itself. And really, the recipe for success in this one was simply time.

*Time.*

Time for others to think about what they'd done. Time for eight-year-old Crystal to grow up to the age of majority and to choose her own future. Time for the brothers to continue their good work, as far as they were concerned. Time for others to act upon what they'd done and to continue with their evil processes, leaving more clues. And time for fear to grow within their hearts.

Doreen stood on the front step, Mugs and Goliath at her side, Thaddeus on her shoulder, the cops still standing around, talking with Mary, Crystal's stepmom, in the back seat of the cop car.

She faced Mack. "I suppose Clara, Crystal's mom, was at the station to give you a statement, wasn't she?"

"She arrived hours ago," he admitted. He looked at Doreen and smiled. "Will you be okay?"

1

"Well, this one has a happy ending, at least," Doreen said hopefully. "You will investigate Crystal's dad and the step-uncles, won't you?"

His face sobered. "We definitely will. And we will bring Crystal back home again."

Doreen smiled. "I can't ask for anything better."

Just then several neighbors approached, while some news vans pulled into the cul-de-sac. Within moments, cameras were rolling.

Doreen groaned. "I guess this will never stop, will it?"

"Not as long as you keep sticking your nose where it doesn't belong," he said cheerfully.

She glared at him. "If a child gets to come home, and several cases get closed, that's good news." Then she smiled up at him. "At least I didn't get hurt this time."

"Good thing," he growled. "You still have stitches in your head from Penny. Could you please try to stay out of trouble for a while? At least until you heal?"

Just then one of the neighbors raced toward Mack, allowing Doreen to sidestep Mack's question. "Hello, hello, police?"

Mack turned to look at him. "Yes, I'm Corporal Mack Moreau. What can I do for you?"

The man held out a paper bag. "You can take this away," he said. "Just a few days ago, I was working in the garden, and I know it wasn't there before then. But I did have somebody run through my yard last Friday night or Saturday morning, it was late, but super early, I don't know … I was asleep and woke up to see him running," he said, the words spilling out of him so fast he was hard to understand.

Mack held up a hand. "Slow down."

"I didn't know what to think of it. I was really nervous."

The neighbor appeared to be in his mid-seventies at least. The small man with a whisper of gray hair on his head scrunched up his face into worry lines. "Here, here, here," he said, shoving the bag at Mack. "Take it."

Mack took the bag and looked inside. His eyebrows shot up toward his hairline, and he said, "Where did you find this gun?"

"That's what I mean. That's what I mean. I was working in the gardenias, and I know it wasn't there before then. But, after that man went through my backyard, I went outside to continue my work the next day, and I found it. I didn't know what to do with it. I thought maybe he would come back and get it again," the man cried out. "So I left it there. It's just me at home, and I knew nobody else would come and take it, but then, when I went out this morning, it was still there. I don't want it. I don't want it," he said, backing up. "You take it."

"Do you have a dark-brown fence?" Doreen asked. "That runs along the creek?"

He turned and looked up. "Yes, yes, that's my place. I see you sometimes walking there."

She nodded. "I love that space. It's a really nice path along the creek."

"Not anymore," he said. "Not anymore." He kept backing away. "Not when people throw guns into my backyard," he said. "This used to be a nice neighborhood." Out came his finger, and he poked it in her direction. "You're the one who keeps bringing all these nasty people here."

She stared at him in surprise. "How is that possible?" she asked. "I'm the one finding and shining the light on all these nasty people who have been living here long before I arrived."

He said, "Well then, you need to find one more. You need to find whoever put that gun in my gardenia patch. It's really not good for the soil." He shot her a hard look, and then he turned and left.

Doreen looked at Mack and said in a conversational tone, "I know who dropped it."

He spun ever-so-slowly, looked at her, and said, "What?"

She beamed up at him. "Maybe we'll have a cup of tea and talk about it on another day. I think I've given you enough work for right now." She motioned toward the chaos. "Definitely another day." And she turned, called the animals to her, and said, "Don't forget. We have a cooking lesson coming up in two days. Mind you get all your paperwork done before then so you can enjoy dinner." With a big smile, she walked inside and closed the door hard.

She leaned against the inside of the door and couldn't stop smiling. Mugs jumped up on his back legs, his front paws hitting her midthigh, and he woofed at her. She reached down and petted him. Goliath, not to be outdone, stretched into the exact same position. She slid down the back of the door until both animals could get at her. Thaddeus hopped up her arm to tuck into the crook of her neck. She cuddled them all and said, "Thank you so very much for saving me again today. And for caring about Mack."

She knew the absolute joy of having all these tomorrows coming to her, even more so now that the animals had saved her life once more. "Treat time," she said.

The animals went crazy. She jumped to her feet, laughing, and said, "You deserve it today, guys. You definitely deserve it today."

As she handed out treats, she couldn't help but think

about the gun in the gardenias and the suspicions she had in the back of her mind. "But that's tomorrow's case," she said, chuckling. "Definitely tomorrow's case."

# Chapter 2

*Thursday Early Morning ...*

**E**ARLY THURSDAY MORNING, Doreen sat outside on the steps of her rear deck with a fresh cup of coffee. She looked across the huge expanse of her garden, loving it, yet, at the same time, hating parts of it. She had a lot of work to be done here, and she never quite seemed to get there. Since she'd arrived in Kelowna, after being replaced with younger arm-candy, her world was not the same. She chuckled. It was, in fact, much, much better. She couldn't believe how much more real it was, and how much more validated and useful she felt. She was doing something with her life now.

Maybe not everybody was happy with what she now did. Lovely Corporal Mack Moreau, the detective she loved to spend time with, made her feel like she was more than a pain in his arse. At the same time though, he liked her enough to give her cooking lessons. She smiled at the thought of their last discussion. She'd basically told him that she had some information about a gun somebody had handed over, then had made it clear she wouldn't even talk to Mack for the rest the day. The last few weeks had been brutal.

She needed a day off for herself. Even a partial day off

would do.

Today she didn't plan to do much besides have tea, rest, and get another ten hours of sleep like she did last night. She felt completely renewed and reinvigorated after her wonderful night. She'd settled into the house finally. It still needed a lot of attention, but the antiques—the furniture, the books, and the paintings—were gone. Now she really wanted to empty out the rest of the house. Put everything in the garage or in the basement or somewhere that would allow her to give the house a spotless cleaning from top to bottom.

She wanted to make sure she got all the corners, nooks, and crannies. She wanted everything found, sorted, tossed, or wiped down. She harked back to the concept of a garage sale. It was either that or maybe several dump runs. Not a whole lot remained in her house though, so maybe it would all go in one trip to the dump. But first she needed food, and she needed more coffee.

She yawned loudly. Mugs, who was lying by her feet on the deck, rolled over and stretched his belly to the sky as she reached out and gave him an extralong scratch. "You were hugely instrumental in saving my life yesterday," she said. "I can't believe how this garden is so lovely, and yet, apparently so lethal."

How many times had she been attacked in her own backyard now? She couldn't even remember. Should she count the newspaper reporter who had accosted her too? As far as Doreen was concerned, that was certainly one negative to her backyard. But Penny? … Well, that went beyond the other assaults. But then again, Penny had attacked Doreen in her own garage. Although Penny may have been momentarily confused because it did look like her old garage. Doreen had moved all of Penny's husband's tools and benches over and had set it up in exactly the same layout.

Wasn't that just so funny? And perfect for Doreen as she now had a great workshop.

Though she wasn't feeling like laughing about Penny now. Not when she was spreading lies about Doreen making up the whole attack story. Penny was causing trouble even from jail. If she was in jail. Maybe she had made bail. Although Doreen hadn't seen any sign of Penny around town. And didn't want to if she was lying about things.

Good thing Doreen had a recording of the event. But who knew she would need something like that? That she would need to legally defend herself after she already had to physically defend herself? She was still thinking about that case. And that hadn't been the last case she'd worked on either.

Doreen still gave Mugs some attention when Goliath, her adopted Maine coon cat, walked across the deck and jumped on her shoulders. He meowed in her ear, his head rubbing along her hair. She put down her coffee cup and reached up so she could scratch his ears and rub Mugs's belly at the same time.

"You were just as helpful too," she said. "I owe you guys big-time."

Just then a squawk came right beside her. "Thaddeus is here. Thaddeus is here."

She chuckled and twisted her head ever-so-slightly so she could see the big African grey parrot she'd inherited from her grandmother, along with the house and Goliath.

"Thaddeus," she said, "you'll have to wait a minute. These guys need some attention too."

The bird turned his head and gave her a glaring look. "Thaddeus is here. Thaddeus is here."

Doreen sighed and had to stop rubbing Mugs's belly in order to gently stroke Thaddeus's chest feathers.

"And you're awesome, Thaddeus," she said with a smile. Then she laughed. How many times had they saved her life already? And who knew, with the trouble she kept getting into, how many more times they would be required to do so? She couldn't imagine life without them anymore. It reminded her of how empty and lonely her previous existence had been. Although married to a megawealthy businessman and hosting a lot of dinner parties and traveling with other social elites, she had been so empty inside. She hadn't even realized it until she had come here.

When her phone rang, she looked at the screen and smiled as she answered. "Good morning, Mack."

"I didn't wake you, did I?" he asked.

She heard the worry in his voice. That added a ray of sunshine to her day. "No, I'm sitting outside on the deck with a cup of coffee," she said. "I think I slept ten hours last night."

"Well, thank heavens for that," he said. "Now, if you would just give yourself a few more days to rest, relax, and unwind, that would be even better. You've had one of the most incredibly chaotic weeks I've ever seen."

"Considering all the antiques moved out of my house and Crystal's case," she said, "I agree. And I have to admit to still being tired. I'm sitting here, feeling mighty peaceful, but, at the same time, I don't really have the energy to get up and grab that second cup of coffee waiting for me."

"So, if I come over right now, I could snag it?"

"I'm pretty sure that, just as you're driving up my driveway, I'll get the energy to steal it in time."

"Wow, that's mean."

"You should probably be making *me* a cup of coffee. How many more cases have we closed?"

"The final details aren't in yet," he said blandly. "A couple cases in Vernon and Kamloops might connect to Crystal's case Mary's brothers traveled all around, building up their collections of sellable items." His tone was wry.

She remembered those *sellable collectibles* were also likely stolen in many cases. "Then your B&E division should be all over this too," she said.

"I think the entire department is. If you're angling for a medal, don't, because that's not something we do."

"No, I can see that. But I just might have a little pull, if I ever need something."

"I hope it never comes to that," he said, "because that's not something we would particularly like to acknowledge. Obviously, if you get into a spot of trouble, and it's innocent and easy-to-fix trouble, the guys can come and help you out. But, if you're expecting to do a crime and go unpunished, no."

She frowned. "You know what? I don't think that's very generous. I mean, look at how many crimes I've stopped. Surely I should be allowed to commit one or two."

"Doreen," he said in warning. "Don't you start …"

She laughed. "See? I caught you."

Mack groaned into the phone. "I'm glad you're in such a great mood this morning," he said. "You know that I'll have to come and take your statement today? And I have to talk to you about something else too."

"The gun," she said. And then she realized she wasn't ready yet. She wanted to sit in the sun, relax, and forget about outstanding cases and getting attacked by people she liked or didn't like, who may or may not have committed crimes. "You're the one who just told me that I needed a week or two to rest."

"No, I said a day or two."

"Then you can come back in a day or two."

"Well, that'll hardly work," he said, "when the gun is sitting here at the station and when I have to put it in evidence and when some of the guys overheard you say that you knew something about it."

She frowned at that. "Did I really open my mouth that loud?"

"Oh, you sure did. The guys have been chuckling since it happened because, in almost every instance, I'm having to talk to you. May have to haul you into the station this time."

"Why?" she asked in outrage. "I only said I knew something about it. I didn't tell you that it was mine."

"No, but considering that we are trying to match the gun with other cases, you can bet, as soon as the results come back, there'll be all kinds of chaos."

"Maybe not," she said. "Who knows just where that gun has been?"

"Exactly. Now, do you want to tell me over the phone, or am I coming over and stealing that coffee?"

"You could try to steal that coffee," she said cheerfully, "but it won't work."

"You want to bet on that?"

At that, she heard her kitchen door slam. She spun around, shocked. Mack stood there, holding a cup of coffee in his hand with a huge grin on his face. She shut off her phone and glared at him. But Mugs, Goliath, and Thaddeus were all over him. She could hardly be mean. Besides, she was delighted to see Mack anyway.

"Now that was a dirty trick," she complained good-naturedly.

"Hardly a trick at all," he said. He reached down and rubbed Mugs's ears. "You owe these guys a lot."

"I know," she said. "It's amazing how protective and how extremely good they are at defending me."

"What's so strange is that they work together. It's one thing for a dog owner to have the dog defend his owner, but it's not just Mugs. It's Mugs, Goliath, *and* Thaddeus. It's like one takes the gun out of your attacker's hand, while the other one knocks him down, and then Thaddeus walks up and down them, pecking away. I mean, it's really bizarre."

"Well, look at that," she said with a grin. "It's almost like you were there."

He chuckled. "It's all good. These guys deserve animal medals."

"Right, and they'll get that, of course," she said, "but I won't get one?"

"Does it matter to you?" He looked at her curiously. "Do you need that form of appreciation?"

"Heavens, no. The last thing I want are more reasons for the media to be all over me. You know what that was like yesterday."

"If you look out front right now …" He gave her a fat smirk. Thaddeus took the opportunity to hop onto his shoulder and cuddle up against his neck. Mack sat on the deck, cross-legged, getting completely covered in dirt. He cuddled the bird. "You really are lucky."

"I know," she said, all her humor fleeing. "Thaddeus is such a cuddle bug, and I had no clue it was even possible." Then she added, "What's out front?"

"If you dare, you can peek around the corner."

She shot him a dark look and sighed knowingly. "It's the media, isn't it?"

He looked at her and said, "Why don't you take a look?"

# Chapter 3

Taking his word, Doreen crept around the side of the house, staying by the fence, until she got to the side where the bushes were. Then she moved into the bushes as far as she could and peered over the fence. And groaned. The entire cul-de-sac was full of TV vans, reporters, and cameramen. It was chaos.

Beside her, behind the fence in the next yard, one of her neighbors growled, startling a shriek out of her. "See? I told you. Neighborhood has gone to pot since you arrived. Why don't you move away and take all those irritating noisemakers with you?"

She didn't turn toward the voice, but she heard the rustle of bushes and then a door slam. She groaned. She would never be friends with her neighbors, would she?

Resigned, she headed back to Mack and said, "The media has completely taken over the road."

"Crystal's disappearance ten years ago made a huge wave across the nation. We had no clue what was going on back then, and now that she's been found ..."

"Have you been in contact with her?" she asked in worry. "I'm not wrong, am I?"

"We spoke with her last night. Her mother has spoken with her too."

"Oh, thank heavens. Can you help her come home?"

"Yes, but we need to get the paperwork for her. Mexico isn't arguing her right to come back to Canada, but we're slowly getting documentation to allow her across the borders."

"Hopefully soon?"

"I would think so. She is a Canadian citizen, and we do have a passport and birth certificate for her. So it's just red tape holding things up."

"Good," she said. "I'd love to meet her."

"I think it's mutual. She's already spoken about you," he said, then gestured to her pets. "She also knows about these guys."

Doreen smiled. "They are definitely part of all this. They were hugely helpful in getting her back and in solving her case."

They sat for a moment in companionable silence. Then Mack said, "So you need to tell me what you know."

"Do I though?" she asked with a teasing but hopeful tinge in her voice. When he didn't respond, she sighed. "You won't leave me alone until I do, so I'll tell you what I know. And, if it's nothing, then it's nothing. Remember Penny's case?"

"How could I forget," he said drily. "Believe it or not it was only a week ago."

"Seriously?" She thought about it and shook her head. "I guess it was. But how crazy is that?"

"It's seriously crazy," he said. "But what about Penny?"

"Remember when I had an intruder one night, and I

chased him down the backyard and up the path?"

He nodded. "As I recall, you didn't say anything to me at the time, only later."

"Yes, and don't go getting angry with me now because it's probably a good thing I didn't catch him," she said. "One of them, whoever that one was—and remember? I said I thought it was two people—one jumped over the fence where this guy lives." She pointed.

"And you thought at that time it was this *Steve* guy, right?"

She nodded and grinned. "See? You do remember."

"What I remember," he growled, "is you went after an intruder on your own at one-thirty in the morning."

"I'm pretty sure it was Penny first. And then Steve was there, and he's the one who jumped over the fence. I presume Penny disappeared in a different direction. That's why I thought the intruder went from small to large. I didn't know if it was due to the shadows or not, but, when he jumped, I thought something was in his hand. Now I'm pretty sure we know who owned the gun. Or at least he had the gun on him when in my neighbor's yard."

"But, if he jumped over the fence, why would he lose the gun?"

"Maybe because, when he jumped, it fell out of his hand, his pocket, his belt, or wherever he was keeping it. It was dark outside, and he didn't dare turn on a light because I'd find him. Plus, somebody from the house might see him, so he took off."

"But wouldn't he have come back the next day?"

"Maybe he did," she said. "And maybe Steve saw the old guy gardening. Who knows? For all we know, Steve might not have remembered which house it was, and he was busy checking the other backyards first."

Mack got up, Thaddeus still on his shoulder. With the dog and cat at his heels, he walked to the end of her backyard.

She followed, knowing he was figuring out how hard it would be to check her neighbors' backyards.

As he stood there, he nodded. "Everybody's got a fence, don't they?"

"Everybody but me now," she said. "Yes."

"So, can *you* point out where the guy jumped the fence?"

Still carrying their coffees, they wandered down the creek.

"That rock was here," she said. "I'll say it was that property."

He pulled up his phone to check something and then nodded. "You're right. That's where the gun was found." Then he glared at her.

She widened her eyes and said, "So now, instead of saying thank-you like any nice gentleman would do, you're mad at me?"

"I'm not mad at you. It just constantly amazes me how you can always be in the middle of trouble."

"I am not in the middle of trouble," she said. "I just gave you a very big lead on yet another case. What does that have to do with me being in trouble?"

"No clue," he said cheerfully. He spun around, hooked an arm around her shoulder, and walked her back toward her house. "I can go to work now and fill out some forms."

"Good," she said, "because I'm tearing the house apart."

At that, he stopped. "What?"

She shrugged. "Everything looks so much better now, but I've still got a lot to sort through. I know that, if I don't get it all done at once, I'll never get it all done. So I thought I would designate one place as a storage area—the basement or the garage probably—and get everything out of *all* the rooms. I'll start cleaning and scrubbing each room from top to bottom too, once everything's been hauled out. Then I'll have a garage sale or will make a dump trip, after I've sorted what I want to keep and see what's left."

"You know what? That's not a bad idea," he said with a grin. Then he shook his head. "That's the problem with moving into an already full house. You have to deal with the stuff still there."

"Exactly, and some of the stuff is definitely old. Maybe not usable and maybe was never usable," she said. "Nobody said Nan was always the most common-sense person."

"Exactly. The dining room should be empty already, isn't it?"

"I think one or two chairs are left. I also think a busted coffee table is downstairs in the basement. I'm not sure. But I want everything out, including the stuff in that root cellar corner. Then I'll make sure there's nothing else to sell so I can finally deal with the last of it."

"That should take at least all day and keep you nicely out of trouble," he said. "I approve."

"Huh, so says you," she said. "For all you know, I could find all kinds of other things down there that send me on more cold cases."

He glared at her. "First, you'll get yourself some food. And then you'll get started. Don't tackle a big job like that without a good meal in you. You're already tired, and your body is stressed, so it needs to be fed properly."

"Speaking of which, you know how to cook pork chops, don't you?" she asked suspiciously.

He chuckled. "I do. And, yes, Friday night, pork chops are on the menu."

"Perfect," she said. "Maybe by then I'll have everything in the garage. I guess some of it will have to go to the dining room and the living room, if I run out of space."

"Make it the dining room," he suggested. "It'll be easier to move the pieces out to the garage from there."

"Good point," she said. Then she walked him through her house and to the front door. She leaned against the porch railing as he backed down the driveway and drove away. All the news vehicles, cameras, and journalists had to move when he backed up. As soon as they realized she stood out here, they turned their attention to her. She rushed inside the house, slammed the door shut, and locked it. Not knowing if anybody would really push the limit, she set the alarm on that door and went back to the kitchen. Now, to prepare an omelet and then get down to work.

# Chapter 4

*Thursday Late Morning ...*

THREE HOURS LATER, Doreen had moved out every unwanted item from upstairs, leaving her mattress on the floor of the master bedroom. But, instead of getting those things as far as the dining room, she only made it to the living room. She had culled out the closets and the bathrooms, and—aside from her toiletries and the clothes she had already sorted in her bedroom and those she had moved to the guest room closet—she completely emptied the second floor.

Deciding that was likely all she could do for the moment, she grabbed the cleaning rags and headed back upstairs, picking the spare room to start on. Although it was full of clothes she still had to decide whether to keep or not, she wiped the shelves and the floors and washed the walls, the doors, the windows, and the ledges.

By the time she had completely finished spring-cleaning all the upstairs, she had a sprawled pile of boxes and containers in her living room. She wiped the stairs as she went down. Then she made a quick trip halfway up to reach for the banister where she had forgotten a couple dusty spindles.

She gave a hearty sigh when she made it back to the first floor. It had taken her longer than she thought, but it was to be expected.

She wondered if she should sort through the piles or keep going. Frowning, she walked into the dining room and found a box of odds and ends. She picked it up and carried it to the living room to add to the rest and cleaned the dining room from top to bottom. She would love to get somebody in here to look at design options with her. She wanted to renovate this room into the open layout she preferred. Still, that was one more room done.

She took a break and made herself a list as she put on the teakettle. Quickly she jotted down what she had done so far and then wrote down the things she still had to do. After that, she walked into the laundry room, which also led to the garage. She had to sort a lot of items here too—boxes of stuff, old coats, and boots. She picked up everything and moved all of it to the center of the garage.

Most of the things left in the garage were junk. She made a second pile in the center for the laundry room contents. That included the laundry soap and all those weird sprays Nan seemed to collect. They made no sense to Doreen. Then she pulled the washing machine and dryer out from the wall, so she could clean behind, finding a dozen odd pieces of lost laundry. She also set the empty washing machine to do a heavy self-cleaning cycle.

With that room sparkling, she walked back to the kitchen. "Well, guys, what do you think?"

They were sound asleep, snoring on the floor, close enough where they could see her, yet far enough they weren't bothered by her multiple *bangs* and *clangs* and moving around of things. She walked out to the garage and looked at the stacks there. She started on the easy things—the laundry soap and that one spray she recognized. She picked those up and put them back on a shelf in the laundry room. And then she studied the rest of the stuff, wondering if she wanted to sort them all right now—which would put her off track—or if she wanted to just continue cleaning the rooms.

Now, however, the trouble was, she had left everything else from the second floor in the living room. That was why Mack had suggested moving everything to the dining room. Or the garage in the beginning. She rolled up her sleeves and transferred everything from the living room out to the garage—except for those two pot chairs. And somehow that was almost symbolic. She walked back in to a fully available living room, outside of that notorious catch-all hall closet. She walked toward it, almost as if she'd never seen it before. Then she opened it, only to be overwhelmed by coats. She groaned and slammed it closed, leaning forward so her forehead rested on the wood. "Oh, Nan," she said. "Just why?"

She opened it again and stared, but there was no help for it. She counted twelve coats in all. There was a rod in the garage. Maybe she would hang these up out there, without sorting through them first, but that would just add to her workload later. She pulled out the twelve coats, laid them over the pot chairs, and emptied one layer from the front closet. More shoes, boots, hats, gloves, and scarves. She put all that into a huge garbage bag and carried it to the garage.

When she returned, she wiped the inside of the closet and the door, leaving the shelves and the stuff stacked in front of the shelves for later today. Otherwise, it was half empty, and, with that, she closed the old hardwood door with a *snick* and turned to face the living room window. The curtains were closed because of the media, but she didn't want to let that stop her. She took the curtains off the rod, rushed to put them into the washing machine. There were enough drapes to do one load. Then she grabbed her glass cleaner and scrubbed the windows. She had done the same upstairs but had forgotten to take down the curtains. She'd do that in a minute.

But, with the living room window cleaned and drape-free, cameras flashed like crazy. She went upstairs and took down all the curtains up there. She made a pile in front of the laundry room so she could put that load on as soon as the first load was done. Then she went to work sorting the coats, moving them to the kitchen table to avoid doing it in front of the bare window.

Before starting, she made herself a big sandwich. She was generous with the ham and cheese for herself and for the critters. Thaddeus thoroughly enjoyed a cherry tomato and some lettuce. She didn't mind that they were eating a lot. She had to keep their energy up, just in case she got into trouble and needed them again.

# Chapter 5

***Thursday Noon ...***

AS SOON AS Doreen finished lunch, she decided to finish scrubbing the living room. So, rather than sorting coats, she returned to the living room, wiped down all the walls, removed everything off the mantel, then finished with a vacuum and a mop of the floor. Now she had everything done except for the hall half-bath, the kitchen, hall closet, and the office corner. But she'd more or less done that alcove when Scott from Christie's had been here with Agatha, his art expert, and John, his books expert.

She walked to the office alcove and saw nothing more to do there except the window, the walls, and the floor. Once she did that, she was down to just the kitchen, the half bath, hall closet, and the garage. It was hard to be upset with her day's work when she'd done a ton already. On that note, she remembered the basement. Groaning, she still had all of that to sort too. But she wasn't sure which way she wanted to go. Her energy was waning.

She walked to the stairs, turned the light on, and headed down to the basement. With a critical eye, she examined what was left on the furniture side and thought about four trips would get it all up to the garage. Then she walked to the smaller area, the cold room, and frowned. Quite a bit of stuff remained on the shelves. Most of it, she didn't think she would keep. She would need more boxes though.

Loading up her arms, she took whatever she could find in the furniture room. Most of these pieces were missing legs. She also found leaves to a dining room table; yet she wasn't sure she still had the table. It took her five trips, leaving a dump run pile at the big garage door, each time bringing an empty box back down with her. Then, with the furniture side done, she walked to the other side and packed up what she could. She would be a couple boxes short. She took these full boxes to the garage—more trash. Then grabbed some big garbage bags for the rest.

By the time the next hour had passed, she was beyond exhausted but had cleared out both sides of her basement. But then she was also euphoric because she had done an incredible amount of work. She needed one more hour in order to get all this cleaned up, but she would need coffee before she did that.

She went upstairs from the basement to the kitchen, put on coffee, dragged a broom and a dustpan along with her cleaning supplies and the vacuum, then did a full sweep-and-vacuum combination of the basement's shelves, doors, stairs, and floors. After that, she wiped down the windows and the walls, and then mopped the concrete floors.

As she dragged her supplies upstairs, she realized she'd forgotten to grab a cup of coffee. But that little pot had been sitting there for a full hour. She groaned. "Way to waste good coffee."

Still, she'd be happy to have it. Besides, she wouldn't let it go to waste. No way she would ruin something like that.

And now the downstairs was done too. She didn't want to think about the garage yet. She'd just moved, hauled, and dumped everything she possibly could in there. Plus, she still had the kitchen to do. With any luck though, that could wait until tomorrow.

She put away her cleaning supplies and poured herself a cup of coffee. Then she checked on the living room window to see if the media was still outside. Of course, they all were. But, as she watched, she saw a young man trying to get through the crowd, carrying a huge box in his arms. He reached her driveway, ignoring everybody behind him.

Doreen watched as the media took shot after shot as the kid came up her front steps. She opened the door to find already three other boxes were here. He dropped that fourth box on top and grinned at her.

"Hi," he said. "I'm Nathan. And these are all for you. Good riddance."

"What? Wait," she said as he raced down the steps. "Hang on!"

He turned and replied, "I want to get out of here before they take any more photos."

"But what are all these things?"

"They're from my great-uncle. You should be expecting them. He's in hospice but wanted to get them out before he died and his files became part of his estate." And, with that, Nathan bolted.

She moved the boxes, groaning at their heavy weight. She stacked them up just inside the front door. And then it clicked who his great-uncle was—Bridgeman Solomon, the journalist. She wanted to cry out in joy, but, at the same time, she expected a single case file on Penny's father and her family. Not boxes and boxes. With everything inside, the front door once again secured, but still hiding from the bare front windows, she headed into the back of the house and switched over the laundry.

She looked at the still-damp curtains and wondered if she could just rehang them. Would the weight help take out the wrinkles? She didn't think she had an iron. And she didn't know how to iron anyway. Knowing her, she would burn them. Taking a chance, she walked back into the living room and used the kitchen step stool to rehang the curtains. With that, she could block out the media.

Satisfied, she pulled them together with a *whoosh* and walked back into the kitchen. This time, she would sit and have her coffee no matter what. But her phone rang as soon as she sat down. She answered it with a groan. "Hi, Mack."

*Silence.*

"Okay, okay," she cried out. "It's been a really busy day."

"I thought you would take it easy today," he said in a stern voice.

"I started cleaning, remember?"

"Is that why you've been busy?"

She heard the relief in his voice and realized he was afraid she had gotten into another case or was racing around terrorizing people again. "Yes, I've done the entire upstairs, basement, and most of the main floor. I only have the kitchen left," she said triumphantly. "Everything else has been emptied, cleaned, dusted, and washed—even the curtains. I dumped the stuff that isn't mine in the garage to sort later."

"Wow." He was silent for a moment before adding, "I'm shocked. But I don't know why. You've already proven you can make incredible progress in a short time."

"Well, I don't know about that," she said, "but this was something I needed to do for a long time."

"Yeah, but go easy on yourself. You have been there six, eight weeks maybe? It's hardly like you've had time to do any major spring-cleaning."

"I know," she said. "And, considering how full this house was when I first moved in, it's looking mighty empty."

"Did you take everything off the walls too?"

"Yes. Pictures, all the kitschy stuff, everything. It's all in the garage. Even the upstairs bathroom was full of all kinds of stuff. Both bathrooms actually."

"Right. I forgot you had a second bathroom up there too."

"Yes, and thankfully the tiny guest bath on the first floor wasn't stocked. So I went right to wiping down the walls and cleaning the floor. Now the whole house looks cleaner, more usable," she said. "Oh, and the bed up there in the spare room really needs to go to the dump, but then I'm sure a bunch of stuff in the garage can join it too. I found a lot of broken pieces of furniture downstairs in the basement, plus leaves from a table. If they don't match anything at this point, I'm hoping maybe a dump run will clean out the rest of it."

"I think that's a great idea," he said in all seriousness. "You've done a fine job there."

"I also found some holes and damaged walls. Some scraped paint, it looks like. I don't know really. It's not drywall down in the basement, but the paneling looks damaged. But then it's old paneling, so I'm not sure if it's real wood or not."

"It's real wood," he said.

She felt like he was smiling as he spoke.

"Back then they didn't know how to fake it like we do today."

She laughed. "So, outside of that, did you have a reason for calling?"

"Yes, one of my men drove past your house today and said it's still a zoo. He thought he saw a kid trying to get through to you but wasn't sure what was going on."

"Oh, that's okay," she said. "And the kid got through."

When she didn't volunteer any more information, he asked in a suspiciously neutral voice, "What kid was that?"

"Oh, just a great-nephew of some guy who's gone from Rosemoor to a hospice."

"Oh. Is that anything I should know about?"

"Of course not," she said blithely. "Did you talk to Steve about his gun yet?"

"No," he said quietly. "But I definitely don't want you talking to Steve."

"I'd be totally happy to never see that man again."

"Well, that's good. Plus, as long as you're housecleaning, that's keeping you out of trouble."

"It is, indeed. Not too much can go on while I'm stuck in the house, can it?"

"Do you want me to shoo away the media?"

"No, leave them, if they haven't got anything better to do," she said, then laughed. "I feel a little sorry for them. It looks like it'll start raining, and that means they'll get soaked in a few minutes. I shouldn't be so mean, but honestly, half the time, I think I should start selling coffee. I'd make a killing."

He laughed. "You know what? You probably would."

Soon afterward Mack hung up, and Doreen sat here, desperately wanting to open the delivered boxes. But she'd promised herself she would do this spring-cleaning job and finish it. The least she could do was go through the twelve coats first. She took one and examined it. It was a long fashionable forest-green trench coat. It was very Avenger-like. She tried it on and laughed. "Nan," she said with a chuckle, "this is seriously gorgeous! I don't know when I'd wear it, but it fits like a charm."

It had a belt, some nice buttons, and a high collar. She shoved her hands into the pockets, surprised they were so deep. Reaching the bottom, she pulled out both hands and put everything she'd retrieved on the kitchen table. Not only was there eighty-five dollars and a bunch of change but also a couple scrap pieces of notepaper, a key, and another one of those weird marble things they had found in the Ming vase. She kept forgetting to ask Nan about them.

She grabbed a bowl from one of the cupboards and put everything in it. Then she searched the trench coat more thoroughly. She found a bunch of business cards in the top pocket and a folded one-hundred-dollar bill that made her cry in delight, rousing the animals to gather around her. Also, a handkerchief that appeared to be silk. She hadn't seen such a thing in a long time. It was embroidered in one corner, but it wasn't Nan's name. It looked like a gentle-man's handkerchief. She thought about Nan's wonderful days and her incredibly exciting single life and thought maybe this was from an admirer.

With that coat thoroughly investigated, including check-ing the lining and the hem of the coat for anything else, she put it back on a hanger and hung it in the front closet. She didn't know if she would wear it much, but it was lovely, and it fit perfectly.

She walked back to the kitchen and grabbed what looked

like a heavy winter coat next. It was very lightweight though and almost reached her midcalf. It was a down coat per the label. Did it get that cold here? She pursed her lips as she studied it. It was a smoky gray color and quite stylish. Nan really did have great taste. Doreen put it on and laughed when she realized she could zip it right up. She couldn't imagine how many times in her life she'd wear it, but, if she needed it even once, maybe it was worth keeping.

Hesitant, yet curious, she shoved her hands into the pockets and cried out when she came up with handfuls again. When she pulled out the items, she found yet another marble. She didn't understand where all these were coming from. She also found more little notes, business cards, and one fifty-dollar bill and one ten-dollar bill. She dumped everything into the bowl to sort later.

Then she took off the coat and went through every pocket, checking the lining and everything else to make sure she hadn't missed anything. She spied a safety pin just under the armpit section and a hole in the lining. It was not very big, but, as she looked closer, she found a one-hundred-dollar bill tucked inside. She stared at it before pulling it out and carefully pinning the area again. She did it in such a way that it was hardly visible. After that, she put the down coat on a hanger and carried it to the front closet. While she was here, she checked the trench coat too, wondering if she'd missed a pin somewhere. But a second check of it showed no such luck.

She had ten more coats to go through. The next two also had money and change, although not of any great denomination—fifteen dollars in one, twelve dollars and forty-six cents in the other. It made her laugh. Then, in the next coat, she found a pair of beautiful heart-shaped earrings. She held them up and wondered how they ended up here. No money was in this coat, just several tissues and a couple business cards. She decided these two coats would go to Wendy, while the coat with the earrings would stay with her. It was a snazzy little blazer that was quite contemporary looking. It hung beautifully on her shoulders too. Her husband would probably call her gaunt, but he liked her that way. The more her collarbones, wrist bones, and rib bones showed, the better for him. She hung up the blazer, then grabbed a big garbage bag to put the coats in for Wendy only they were so big, she ended up just stacking them instead.

With that done, she had seven more coats. One was a raincoat, and nothing else was in it other than a walnut. She didn't understand why, but then she was past wondering. Meanwhile, another coat had a lovely little stone. As she looked at it, it flashed many colors, like a raw opal. She shrugged and put in it the bowl, along with one hundred and nine dollars and forty-one cents.

By the time she was done, she had one more jacket she could wear every day, and the bowl was almost full of odds and ends. She was now left with five coats to keep and seven to give away. She placed the coats in front of the big garage door. She would have to put them in her car, but that meant going outside and facing the media world again. She wasn't up for that yet. She also had a pile of other stuff stacked in the garage anyway. Stuff she had yet to get rid of.

One day she'd finally be rid of it all. Someday …

# Chapter 6

*Thursday Afternoon ...*

FINALLY, DOREEN COULDN'T stand it anymore. With another cup of coffee, she headed for the four boxes in the living room delivered earlier today. The only things left in the living room were the two pot chairs and these boxes. She dragged one of the chairs to the stacked pile and opened the top box. Apparently, the files were alphabetized, and this was the first group. The next box had letters *P* through *Z*. She shook her head. Sighing, she put the boxes side by side on the floor. Then she went to Penny's family name. Sure enough, there was a file. She read it and found it very interesting and also sad.

Penny's brother had gone through a tremendous amount of abuse from their father, yet their case always seemed to slip through the cracks, and the brother was never removed from the home. Doreen wondered why Penny herself didn't say anything to anyone, but it was always hard to judge the veracity of a child who was also in the same situation—and likely terrified too. At least their father had eventually gone to trial, and Penny had been brave enough to testify against him.

That racked Doreen with guilt even more. Penny hadn't had an easy time in her childhood. She had stood up for her brother, and she had done what she could. But then she had killed her brother in an effort to save him from that life, and her father had done time for the murder she had committed. Without a doubt, he deserved jail time for what he had done to his children, but he hadn't been the one guilty of the final offense.

Reading to the end of Penny's file, Doreen didn't find much new information. She set it aside though, planning to scan it in for her own permanent records and then possibly give Mack the original or a scanned set of copies. She'd have to think about that. Putting this file back in the proper place, she stared at the four boxes from Solomon. An astronomical amount of files were here. The old man had been a journalist, but it didn't mean he had followed only criminal cases or that these were unsolved cases. She pulled out her phone. "Good afternoon, Nan," she said.

"About time you called me. Did you know this place is buzzing like crazy?"

"My front yard too," Doreen said sadly. "The media is walking all over the lawn."

"You get them off the grass. We've been through that before."

"A lot of them are out there. Mack told me how Crystal's disappearance had caused so much pain for everybody and how the whole community had banded together to search for her when she first went missing. And now that they know Crystal's alive and well and coming home ..."

"You are a true hero, my dear," Nan said warmly. "You should hear everybody talk."

"I'd just as soon not," she said. "But thanks. How is Solomon doing?"

"He's still alive," Nan said in a cheerful voice. "I think he's doing it just to spite his family. Right now they're arguing about the financial assets he's leaving behind."

Doreen winced at that. "That's terrible. People should let him die in peace."

"Or he should have given it all away before he got to that stage, like I'm doing with you."

"Speaking of which," Doreen said, then proceeded to explain everything she did this morning.

"Oh my, I bet the house looks wonderful."

Doreen looked around the mostly bare living room. "Well, it definitely looks different. I haven't done the kitchen yet, and I'm still working on the hall closet now."

"Oh, that closet," Nan said. Worry coated her voice. "I have to admit, it's very deep and pretty stuffed."

"Stuffed with what?" Doreen asked with dread.

"You'll find out," Nan said in her usual singsong voice.

"Oh, by the way, Solomon's great-nephew finally got the files to me." There was silence for a moment, as if Nan struggled with the change of topic. Doreen added, "The file on Penny's family."

"Oh, my goodness, it's not like you need them now."

"No, but I think it'll be helpful for Mack. Maybe helpful for Penny's defense too. She had a terrible childhood. I've been reading bits and pieces of it, and she went through a lot of trauma and abuse. I almost feel guilty."

"And believe me, the defense will play that up big-time, so you don't need to," Nan said. "She tried to kill you. Remember that."

"And she did kill her brother, and she shot Hornby," Doreen said. Then she smiled before continuing, "The thing is, the nephew brought me that file as part of a bunch of files. He brought me four large boxes *full* of files."

Nan gasped, then laughed.

"It's hardly funny! I just cleaned out the house, and now I'm sitting here with four large boxes full of paperwork."

"Yes, but just think about how many cases are in those boxes!"

"Sure, but that doesn't mean they're unsolved or have anything to do with me. I understand it's part of Solomon's legacy, but I don't know what I'm supposed to do with them."

"I might pop by and talk to him this afternoon," Nan said. "They let me in there a couple days ago. If they do again, I can ask him. It'll depend on how many watchdogs he has around."

"If you wouldn't mind, that would be helpful. See if any of these cases still really bother him or if there's something I'm supposed to do. If it's just his old journalistic research, it's probably not worth keeping. And, of course, I appreciate Penny's file because that would be helpful for moving the court case forward, but the rest …"

"Don't you worry about it. I'm on it." With that, Nan hung up.

Just then though Doreen received another phone call. She groaned. "You know that I could rest more if I didn't have interruptions all the time."

"Darren says you got a delivery today," Mack said, ignoring her jibe.

"Who's Darren again?"

"Richie's great-grandson," he said. "The one we met at Rosemoor when Nan and Richie got into trouble, and the police were called. You said a kid got through the crowd to you, but you didn't say what he was delivering." His voice was too suspicious for her.

She wrinkled her nose. "Did Darren tattle on me?"

"Why would he tattle?" Mack asked, his voice looming with worry. "What are you up to?"

"Well, somebody who's in hospice—that journalist fellow—sent his nephew with the case file for Penny, which I knew was coming but didn't receive in time to help us since Penny attacked me soon afterward." The words rushed out. "Anyhow, Solomon wanted to get rid of his research files before they became part of his estate and became something else for his lawyers and his heirs to haggle over. That was what the kid brought me through the media barricade today."

She stared at the files as she talked to Mack, then saw a note tucked in the front of one of them. She pulled it out. "Oh," she said. "He's gifted them to me, according to this note. The handwriting is pretty rough and scrawled, but I imagine it goes along with the fact that he's probably feeling pretty rough. It does say, 'Dear Doreen, here is my life's work. Hopefully it will help you on yours.' And it's signed *Solomon*."

"On yours?" Mack asked. "Since when is solving cases your life's work?"

"I don't know," she said dismissively. "Who knows what Nan's told him?"

"Or who knows what he's deduced himself," Mack said. "I highly doubt any of that material is of any value."

"You might want to see Penny's folder though. I read some interesting tidbits. There is nothing new, but it proves she had a terrible childhood. It also has clippings of what Solomon found throughout the years on her case."

"Well, maybe I'll take a look. If nothing else, we should probably have it for our file and to share with the prosecutor."

"Exactly. It'll be better if he knows what the defense lawyer knows as well."

Mack laughed. "Now you're even starting to think like a cop. Lord help us."

"But I don't know if any of the rest of these files are of interest or not," Doreen said. "Did you get anywhere on that gun?"

"No, we're still waiting for the ballistics report."

"Interesting. On that note, do you remember what Steve's last name was?"

"Albright."

She went to the boxes. "Aha!"

"What does that mean?" Mack asked, his voice rising.

"There's a folder with that name on it."

"Doreen," he said in warning, "don't you dare go down that path."

She chuckled. "How can I not? Somebody has gifted me with his whole life's work of research on criminals. You should see how thick *this* file is."

"Well, Steve Albright's a corporate lawyer. Of course, it'll be thick. That doesn't mean it's anything criminal."

"I know," she said, "but I'll have fun taking a look anyway." As soon as she said that, she ended the call, picked up the huge file, and walked into her kitchen. Then she groaned. She still had so much to do in the kitchen, but her energy had completely died now. She dropped the file atop the kitchen table and turned to her pets. "What do you guys want to do?"

Mugs woofed at the door. They probably needed to go

out. They hadn't had any exercise today. She was the one who had worked her butt off, scrubbing, cleaning, and making several trips up and down the stairs. They hadn't. She picked up a mug and poured the last of the coffee in it. "How about a trip to the creek then?"

She opened the door and let the animals out but remembered something. The media was around, and she had all those files in her house. She went back to the front door, reset the alarm, and rushed to the kitchen to set that alarm too before heading outside.

Nan texted just then. **No luck. Too many watchdogs.**

At that, Doreen interpreted the conversation to mean Nan couldn't get in to see Solomon. She quickly responded, **Don't worry about it. It's fine.**

Her mind buzzed, and she wondered what she should do. Somehow she had to keep the boxes safe. She didn't want anybody to know she had them. That thought came too late because she'd already told Mack and Nan. Mack wouldn't blab, but he would want to see them. And Nan? … Well, the truth was, Nan *would* blab. And, sure enough, it would be Doreen who got into trouble.

With that thought, Doreen didn't take too long with her walk of her animals along the creek. Plus Doreen's muscles ached. She turned her brood around and headed for a hot shower and then to bed early tonight.

# Chapter 7

*Friday Morning ...*

DOREEN WOKE UP, rolled over, and groaned. Who knew cleaning a house would cause her body so much physical stress? Somehow she had been cocky and had thought last week's work in Penny's garden had toughened her up. But Doreen still hadn't used her muscles enough to handle this kind of regular activity. As she remembered all the loads she had taken from upstairs down and from downstairs up, she realized she really did deserve to be sore today. On top of that, she had scrubbed everything in the house except for the kitchen and that hall closet. She was determined to do them so she could count the job as done. Then winced because she still had the entire garage to look after too.

Goliath jumped on the bed just then and nudged her in the face with his forehead. That big guttural purr of his demanded attention. She was more than happy to give it to him.

With both hands, she gently scrubbed up and down his neck, around his ears and cheeks, and above his forehead. Then she gave him long, smooth strokes down his back and along his tail. He stretched out fully, his tail swishing back and forth. He kept hitting Mugs's face with it. And likely on purpose. He ended up waking Mugs, who rolled over. Then the next time his tail came by, Mugs opened and clamped his mouth on it fast. Goliath screeched and turned to Mugs. In an instant, a chase ensued. They ran down the hallway and into the other bedroom and then finally back around again and down the stairs.

Doreen groaned at the noise because Mugs wouldn't stop barking, and Goliath was letting him know exactly what he thought of this treatment. But though Goliath had chased Mugs out of her bedroom, it was Mugs who chased Goliath back in. She laughed.

"You guys are just doing this for fun," she said. She sat up on the bed and looked around her clean room, smiling. She still had the weird hanger contraption she'd created and hung from the ceiling for Thaddeus to roost on. Thaddeus rested gently on it, watching the critters race. She walked to the bird and cuddled him. Immediately he threw himself sideways into the palm of her hand. She picked him up and held him against her chest.

"Thaddeus is here," he said. "Thaddeus is here."

She chuckled and lifted him higher, then kissed him on his neck. "And Doreen is delighted that Thaddeus is here."

Gently he moved up her shoulder, where he nestled against her hair. Even those subtle moves caused her pain. Since she had already had a hot shower last night, she would take a muscle relaxant this morning. She got dressed, easily finding something new to wear from Nan's stack she'd kept for herself. She didn't have many belongings to begin with, so it was a shock to uncover Nan's eclectic fashion collection. Even after paring down her clothes a great deal, a lot still occupied a whole spare room. Things Doreen now had to inspect once more to see if she'd keep them or not.

With Thaddeus still on her shoulder, she walked downstairs to the kitchen, disabled the alarms, opened the kitchen door, and watched as the cat and dog raced through the doorway to the backyard. She laughed as she stepped outside to see the morning sun dappling across her lawn.

"Good morning, world," she cried out happily. It really was a lovely day. Nobody was after her. As far as she knew, everybody involved in something nasty was in jail, and her day was her own. Of course, she had those files from Solomon, but she would look into them more before Mack arrived. He'd promised to come and cook pork chops tonight. She did want to have a full digital copy of everything made, just in case Mack had designs on those boxes.

With that thought in mind, she put on coffee, grabbed the big file on Penny and stacked up as many of the like-minded pages as she could, then ran them through her scanner. By the time that file was done, so was the coffee. She renamed the PDFs and sent one copy to Mack and saved one for herself. After that, she returned the folder to the box and carried her coffee outside.

Goliath and Mugs ran in circles beside her, while Thaddeus chirped in a happy and lively tone. Smiling, Doreen walked to the creek and stuck a bare toe in it. "*Brr*," she said. "Hardly swimming weather."

"Thaddeus likes water. Thaddeus likes water."

"You do, indeed," she said. She lifted him off her shoulder and set him on one of the big rocks right against the shore. "Now you can sit there and watch the water go by," she said.

Instead of watching though, he went to the other side of

the rock where it sat in the creek and dipped his head for a drink.

She picked him up again after he drank, then walked farther down the creek. Her other two critters followed her. It was a seriously gorgeous day. As she got closer to the water, she kicked off her flip-flops and stepped into the cool water fully this time. "Cold but lovely," she repeated with a smile.

"Thaddeus likes water," the bird murmured against her ear. "Thaddeus likes water."

"Do you want to sit on the rocks?"

His head bobbed up and down, his feathers fluffing out then flattening again. She knew he had a complex language for every movement he made, but she didn't really understand all his nuances. She helped him off her shoulder and then carefully placed him on one of the bigger flat rocks in the creek. He could still walk back to dry land if he wanted to. Immediately though, he went to the shallow end and bent his head for another sip of cool water.

"Tastes good, doesn't it?" she asked him.

But he was too busy drinking to respond. Then he pecked at some unseen object on the rock, completely happy. Doreen looked at Goliath, laying on the path with his tail flicking as he watched Thaddeus. She could almost see the thoughts the cat had. He was thinking the bird was *crazy*. Meanwhile, Mugs seemed to take great delight in just bouncing around. But then he backed up, took several stiff-legged hops and flew into the water. He sent a wave crashing toward Thaddeus, who squawked and flapped his wings. The bird stumbled backward before righting himself. After that, he proceeded to rip into Mugs and to tell him off fiercely.

Doreen laughed. "I know it's bad to laugh at you," she

said, "but you guys really do keep my life fun and exciting."

"Just make sure you keep it that way," a man's hard voice said behind her. "Because snooping around in other people's business will cut short that little idyllic scene of yours."

She stiffened but didn't bother turning around. She already recognized the voice. "Good morning, Steve. Still out to cause trouble?"

"You're the one causing trouble. I've hired an excellent criminal lawyer for Penny. You'll rue the day you made up those stories."

"I didn't make anything up," she said. "Good for you for helping your friend out though. After all, I'm sure she didn't really mean to kill her brother or to attack Hornby or me."

"It's all lies," he said.

"So, I take it you were lovers," she said in a conversational tone. "There's really no other reason to continue to defend her, even in the face of all the evidence."

An ugly silence came before he responded. "And now you impinge her honor. You might be so low but I am not."

"Interesting turn of phrase, so you loved her, but from a distance," Doreen said with a laugh, turning to look at him.

He was dressed in an all-black getup, and his hands were in his hoodie pockets. It was like one big kangaroo pocket, and she worried about the possibility of him having a gun in there. She always wondered why people pulled a gun out of a pocket when they could shoot right through it.

An awkward silence followed while they stared at each other. "She's been keeping secrets from you."

Something baleful was in his gaze. "I'm a corporate lawyer. I have all kinds of secrets I keep for my clients."

"Right, because corporate lawyers do that. They help

corporations save money. And they cheat and steal too."

"No, we don't," he bit off. "And I won't have you tarnishing my reputation. That's called slander."

"Right, it's all about your reputation, isn't it? I wonder how your reputation will hold up, knowing you were caught running through my backyard with a gun—then losing said gun—for the cops to find?" When she caught the shock in his face, she nodded slowly. "Did you really think I wouldn't recognize you?"

He took a step back.

"Yeah, you better keep going," she said. "I know you're in cahoots with Penny. The question is, will you be up for charges as a coconspirator to attempted murder?"

"You've got it all wrong," he stated with a shake of his head.

"What I don't have wrong is the fact that you were trespassing on my property with a gun. I chased you to the creek. Penny went one direction, while you went the other. It was pretty obvious who you both were. And then, like an idiot, you lost the gun." She paused before adding, "You do know it's been handed in to the cops?"

She'd never seen a man go as pale as a ghost. She had heard the phrase many times but had never actually seen it. She nodded slowly. "You better have an explanation," she said, "and fast. The police will be knocking on your door soon."

"I had nothing to do with anything," he spat out.

"Well, good. Then why are you so terrified?"

He shook his head again. "You don't know anything. And your interference is ruining everything. Stop meddling in people's lives. You don't understand."

"Help me understand then," she said in a coaxing manner. "Seriously. Help me. I don't understand how you're as sweet and innocent as you keep trying to tell me when you were trespassing with a gun, which means you had an intent to murder someone." She knew she was making up some of the legal terminologies because what did she know? She just liked to watch cop shows. That didn't mean she understood the language. But then she studied Steve's body language and nodded. "You're terrified about something. I highly suggest you go back and think about where you stand in all this and just what trouble you might be in for real now."

"For real?" he asked mockingly. "What are you, sixteen?"

"Not even close," she said. "But I will admit, on days like today, I do feel like I'm sixteen. It's lovely. It's also weird and awkward too. But then again, you've got to be at least fifty-eight—or maybe a year or two younger but not by much. Maybe you were Penny's younger lover. Who knows?" She shrugged. "I can't be too bothered about your sex life."

He mumbled under his breath with another shake of his head. And then, when he didn't have anything else to say, the normally very articulate Steve spun on his heels and almost ran up the path. Doreen watched him go and wondered if she should add something, like a snappy retort.

But nothing came to her mind much less to her tongue. What she really wanted was to yell at him to stay away. But he was already so far gone that he wouldn't have heard her.

Belatedly she noted how her animals had rallied about her. Goliath had gotten up and sat down beside her, staring as Steve raced away. Mugs no longer splashed carefree in the water either. He instead stood beside her with the back of his neck all bristled. Even Thaddeus had crossed the creek to be nearby.

She reached out a hand on either side and gently stroked both pets. "He's gone for now, guys. Let's hope he stays away."

# Chapter 8

*Friday Midmorning ...*

SLOWLY DOREEN WANDERED back to the house and wondered if she should tell Mack about Steve. She'd already emailed him earlier, but it made sense to double-check if he was coming for pork chops tonight. Just the thought of barbecue pork chops—well, maybe not barbecue since she didn't have a barbecue pit—or any version of pork chops made her mouth water. Without questioning herself, she hit the speed dial for Mack and waited for him to answer. His answering machine got the call instead. Frowning, she wondered if that meant he was in a meeting or if he was off on another case.

The thought of being on another case so soon almost filled her with fatigue. At the same time though, her interest spiked. Since Crystal's case potentially connected to however many more cases, Mack could still have a mess of paperwork to do, interviews to attend, and loose ends to tie up in each and every one of those cases. He was probably too darn busy to answer the phone. She hung up without leaving a message.

Her phone rang as she walked to her small deck. It was

Mack's mother, Millicent.

"Could you please come tomorrow instead of today?" Millicent asked fretfully. "I do love your visits, but I have to go out this morning for doctors' appointments. I'd prefer to stay home, but I have to go see them."

"Oh, no problem," Doreen said gaily. "I can come Saturday morning. Not an issue." Mentally she was pleased to have the spare time today. It would allow her to work on her house instead.

Inside now, she settled on toast with cheese for her breakfast and then walked into the living room and stared at the boxes of folders. If she got into those, she would never finish the kitchen. She wanted the kitchen done before Mack got here for dinner tonight. So she pushed the boxes of files farther along the wall to the side of the front door, so Mack wouldn't trip as he stepped inside with his hands full of grocery bags, blocking his view of the floor.

Then, with a cleared space, she emptied everything from the kitchen into the living room. It was the only way she could sort through it all. She started with the cupboards under the stove and worked her way all the way around. By the time she had everything emptied, Thaddeus sat on top of the turkey roaster. He squawked at her, and she smiled.

"Better watch it," she said. "I might get ideas if you sit on that."

He squawked again, then flapped his wings, and hopped off. She chuckled and came back with another load of baking dishes of all shapes and sizes. She'd love to learn how to bake, but, at the moment, all cooking was just this big mystery. Plus, some of these pans looked like they had big holes in them. She didn't understand what they were for. They didn't look like muffins or doughnuts. It said "cake pops" on the side. She shook her head, not knowing what that was or why Nan would care. By the time Doreen was done moving everything, once again her living room was full of stuff. She groaned. "Nan, this is ridiculous! You collected way too much stuff. Especially considering you hardly ever cooked."

But, with that done, she scrubbed all the cupboards both inside and outside, the countertops, and the windows. The fridge itself was mostly empty, but she gave it a good scrub too. The only item she didn't scrub was the stove, as it was brand new. So she had the floor and the window by the table to clean next.

When she was done, she stood here, mop still in hand, and smiled at her critters. "Ta-da," she said. "I'm done!"

She went to put away her cleaning supplies, remembering she still had the rest of that front hall closet to do. She looked back at the living room and all the canned food and dishes she had to sort through and shrugged. Better to get it all out now. Whether she sorted the contents right away or not, at least she would have everything finally emptied out of all the rooms and all the closets and all the cupboards. Thankfully she had already done the pantry when Scott was last here.

It took an incredible number of trips to empty the hall closet and set it all on the living room floor. She separated this pile to one side. That closet was deep. She knew Nan had warned her, but holy crap.

An ancient vacuum cleaner was in the back. When she pulled it out, she found another sad-looking vacuum behind it. This one was a ball-like thing with lots of hoses attached. It looked like something out of a science fiction movie. Finally, the closet was empty. Yet, as she looked at the shelves, she groaned. It looked like they were all stained. She went back to the kitchen and grabbed what she needed, then started scrubbing. When she got up on a step stool to reach the top shelf, she found another attic doorway too. She'd already been up in the attic through the spare bedroom, so she had no clue where this led to. She looked closer and realized it led under the stairs.

Frowning, she opened it by sliding the wood hatch to the side. It was awkward because it was above the top shelf in this closet. As she tried to get up higher on the step stool, she realized the shelves came out.

"Doreen, you're an idiot," she announced to anyone who cared to listen. Then she stepped back to the floor and removed the shelves completely, putting them in the kitchen so she could wipe them later, and moved the step stool inside the closet and grabbed her phone with its flashlight app to check what was up above. She found boxes. Boxes and boxes of boxes. She stared in dismay, wondering what the devil could possibly be in them. Then, as if understanding what she was up to, her phone rang. She switched it out of Flashlight mode to answer the call. "Good morning, Nan," she said.

"Oh, my dear," Nan said. "It's almost noon."

Doreen groaned. "I know, but I decided I would finish this job once and for all."

"What job?" Nan asked in a perky tone. "Did you get another job? That's wonderful to hear."

"No," Doreen said. "I'm cleaning everything inside the house. I just emptied all the cupboards and cleaned them along with the counters in the kitchen. I'm doing the last part of the house now, which is the hall closet. I've got it completely emptied out, and I was cleaning it when I found this little trapdoor hatch above it.”

“Is there?” Nan asked with curiosity. “What’s up there?”

Doreen stared down at the phone. “Nan, I think I’m supposed to ask you that question.”

“I don’t know,” Nan said in a testy voice. “It’s almost as if you expect me to remember everything I did in that house over the last forty-odd years.”

“Sorry. I might be a little tired.”

“Time for another pot of coffee,” Nan announced. “Really, you should take better care of yourself, dear.”

“I’m trying. That’s why I’m doing this. So I can get everything cleaned up and feel good about it.”

“That’s one way to look at it,” Nan said. “But I think you should leave everything and come here for lunch.”

“Lunch?” Doreen asked hopefully. “Why lunch?”

“Because we took a trip to the German bakery and delicatessen this morning. You know the one off Capri and Sutherland?”

“Sure, I know that one. But I’ve never been in it. I assumed it was expensive.”

“Of course, it’s expensive.” Nan laughed. Her voice was more of a trill than anything this morning. “But they have lovely stuff anyway. I picked up some really good rustic bread and bought meat and cheeses. I’m about to make a salad and some sandwiches. I want you to come and share the feast with me.”

“I’d love to,” Doreen said, casting a glance at the living room.

“No buts,” Nan stepped in. “You can continue with all that when you get back.”

“You’re right.” And then her stomach growled.

Nan laughed, apparently hearing the sound. “It sounds

like you need to come soon. That stomach of yours is empty."

"I'll be there in a little bit," Doreen said. She hung up and studied the boxes in the attic again, but she couldn't even begin to reach them. She'd need a ladder. Or someone tall. And, of course, on that note, she thought of Mack, who was coming tonight for pork chops. She clambered off the stepstool, surveyed everything she had done up until now and smirked with satisfaction. "I may not have gotten you all sorted yet, but I feel proud."

For half of the kitchen stuff though, she might need Mack's help to tell her if she should keep any of this. Who knew how old some of the kitchen items were and what she'd do with them? Then there were the canned goods. … She'd never heard of canned potatoes before. She walked back into the kitchen, washed up, and then ran upstairs to the bedroom to switch out of her dirty clothes. She came back down to find the animals staring at her from the bottom of the stairs. She grinned. "You guys want to go to Nan's?"

Mugs woofed and headed for the front door. She called them back. "Let's go by the creek," she said. "Come on." But first, she checked to make sure the front door alarm was still set and locked the back door. Then she headed to the creek to visit with Nan. It was one of the best parts of living here.

Rekindling that relationship hadn't seemed important before, but that was when she had lived differently. It went along with that empty and hollow person she had been who didn't know right from wrong apparently. If she understood one thing now, it was how wrong it was to have ignored Nan. And how absolutely right it is to have her as close and as loving as she is now.

# Chapter 9

*Friday Noon …*

THE ANIMALS KNEW the way to Nan's home as well as Doreen did. And apparently, they were eager to head in that direction too, especially Goliath and Mugs. Doreen was hard-pressed to catch up, but so was Thaddeus. Finally, he flew ahead of the others, only to almost get overrun. She chuckled and bent down, offering him the back of her hand. He hopped on without hesitation.

"I know you want to walk with us, big guy," she said, "but sometimes it's just easier if you go with the flow."

He crooned against her head gently, almost dumping himself sideways so he was lying down.

She smiled and cuddled him. "We'll go see Nan, Thaddeus."

"Thaddeus loves Nan," he said on a croon. "Thaddeus loves Nan."

Doreen laughed in delight. "I've never heard you say that before! I sure wish I could tape you when you talk like that." Then she urged him, "You want to say it again?"

But, of course, Thaddeus gave no answer. As they came around the corner, Mugs and Goliath ran across the stepping stones to greet Nan, who was waiting for them. Doreen smiled as Nan crouched to cuddle both animals. By the time she arrived at Nan's side, Nan was laughing and sitting on the flower box as she tried to give each equal attention.

"It doesn't work, you know?" Doreen said with a chuckle. "No matter how much you give them, they'll want more. And, as soon as you try to be fair, they'll immediately feel like it isn't fair. You just can't win."

"Maybe not," Nan said with a lovely smile. "But it's a wonderful way to lose." She gave each of them a kiss on top of the head and straightened up. She then gave Doreen a big hug and reached up to spend a moment with Thaddeus. That wasn't enough for Thaddeus either. He walked across onto Nan's hand and then up her arm to sit at her shoulder, where he tucked up against the crook of her neck. Nan spent a moment with her eyes closed, holding him against her.

"I can't forget all you," she said. "I don't think I can ever get enough of these guys."

"I'm sorry you can't have any of them here," Doreen said.

"It's one of those nasty little regulatory rules," Nan said. "And sometimes I'm fine with that, but then I just miss them so much." She opened her eyes. "But that's enough about this. Lunch is ready."

Doreen gasped when she looked where Nan pointed behind her. "Wow, this looks lovely." There were thick slabs of some chewy bread with a plate full of meat, pickles, cheeses, tomatoes, and vegetables, like cucumbers, off to the side. "This is a great spread, Nan."

"And I didn't want to sit here and eat it alone. Let's eat and have a cup of tea afterward."

So that was what they did. After her first slice of bread,

Doreen marveled at how simple yet fulfilling a meal like this could taste. When she mentioned it to Nan, her grandmother said, "I was afraid you wouldn't really want to come for such simple fare."

"Different bread, different meat, different cheeses," Doreen said with a chuckle. "I've never had all of it at once. And I'm very short on pickles too." She picked one up, took a bite, and shook her head at the unusual explosion of flavor. "What are these?"

"Gherkins," Nan said. "Didn't your husband like pickles?"

Doreen shook her head. "No pickles. He wasn't into vinegar. We did have olives though. We always had multiple kinds of olives."

"That's fine and dandy," Nan said with a sniff, "but pickles are cheaper."

"I haven't bought any olives since I left," Doreen said. "But, if these are cheaper, I'll consider getting some."

"Did you find anything interesting when you went through the kitchen?"

"All kinds of things *called* interesting," Doreen said with a smile. "I didn't know what half of those pans and cooking dishes were. And, right at the moment, everything is stacked up in the living room."

"That must be a huge pile."

"Well," Doreen said, "let me rephrase that. Everything from the kitchen and the hall closet is in the living room, while everything else from the house is out in the garage. I'm not sure how long it'll take to sort through those piles. I'll do the kitchen and hall closet first though, and then maybe this weekend I'll tackle that pile in the garage."

Nan brightened up. "Oh, before I forget," she said,

"have you found your next case from Solomon's files?"

"Not necessarily," Doreen said slowly, not wanting to even speculate if Steve's gun was a case she could work on. "But you never know."

"Exactly," Nan said. "I figured there would be all kinds of things that could get you into a lot of trouble."

"Yeah, and you think there's just one file," Doreen said. "You're not allowed to share all this, but I have four boxes full of files."

Nan clapped her hands in delight. "Solomon and I had talked about it earlier, but I didn't know it was so much."

"There's a lot of information, so it'll take me a long time to go through them."

"But you'll take the time," Nan said. "I know you'll do them justice."

"Doesn't mean there's anything to find though," Doreen said. She picked up a piece of cheese and took a bite, then closed her eyes. "This is a lovely Gruyère."

"I remembered you loved it," Nan said complacently. "And sure, it's expensive, but it's worth getting."

At that, Doreen reached for a second piece, waggling her eyebrows at Nan. They enjoyed lunch, and, by the time they were done, not much food was left except for a piece of ham for Mugs and a piece of cheese for Goliath, who tossed it around on the floor like it was a mouse. Meanwhile, Thaddeus helped himself to a slice of tomato. Then, with the table cleaned off, they put on the teakettle.

As Doreen sat, Nan came back out with a plateful of something luscious looking, topped with chocolate and filled with cream. Doreen smiled. "You know what?" she said. "I thought I was full, but I guess I'm not quite that full."

"These were freshly made this morning. Let's enjoy

them."

"Exactly."

By the time they were done, Doreen was thoroughly full and completely satisfied and content. "Now," she said, "if I could just go home, sit by the creek, and read a book."

"Do it," Nan urged. "There's nothing else in your life right now. You don't have to work like a slave all day again."

"No," Doreen said with a sigh. "I want to get the house done before I dive into Solomon's files. So much information is there, but, if I stop what I'm doing, I'll never get the spring-cleaning done. And I'm determined to finish the sorting and that cleaning."

Nan shook her head. "You are very focused, my dear. I hear you found somebody's gun too."

"Yes, a few houses up from my place."

Nan nodded. Then, a crafty gleam in her eyes, she asked, "Whose was it?"

"No clue but I might know who threw it there."

At that, Nan pulled out her pen and a pad of paper, picked up her eyeglasses sitting off to the side, then wrote down a few notes. "Details, details," she told Doreen. "I need details, my dear."

Doreen told her what she knew, which wasn't much.

Nan's lips went into an *O* shape, and she sat back. "Now I know why you want to go home and get into Steve's file," she said. "I thought this all had to do with Penny."

"I scanned in all of Penny's file and sent it to Mack already. He'll see that whoever needs it gets it."

"Did you read it?"

"I did," Doreen said. "But it's not a nice read. It was very sad." She sighed. "Penny had a terrible childhood, and I think a sympathetic jury will let her off with just a light sentence."

"But she attacked you," Nan said in outrage. "And she shot Hornby."

"True," Doreen said. "And she'll probably end up serving time for both of those actions, but I don't think it'll be that much. On top of that, most of the jury will be very compassionate about what she did for her brother."

Nan nodded slowly. "That's a tough one."

"I can't help but think she should have gone to the police about her brother instead though. She should have helped him out of that house and called somebody because she was the older sister. She should have done something more."

Nan's finger came out and wagged at her.

Doreen agreed. "I know I shouldn't be so judgmental. I understand she was just as terrified as everybody else, but a part of me wonders if she didn't do it just to make sure her father got caught."

At that, Nan frowned. "I never even thought of that. The way your mind works, dear …"

Doreen shrugged as she sipped from her teacup. "I'm not even sure it works well. It just vomits out ideas."

"Oh," Nan said with a laugh. "I do love talking with you. Such fun!"

# Chapter 10

*Friday Midafternoon ...*

IT WAS MIDAFTERNOON when Doreen headed for home, and she felt pleasantly content. The work on her home was the last thing on her mind because Nan had now spiked Doreen's interest in Steve's folder again. But then she was a little worried somebody would come along and steal the file before she had a chance to scan it. That was a pressing reason for finishing her housecleaning job. That would make it so she could get those boxes into that hall closet and out of sight. Frowning, she let herself into the kitchen but decided she was too full for another cup of tea. She'd wait until Mack got here and would fix coffee.

She walked into the living room and groaned. There was so much to deal with. She started with the dishes and selected herself a matching service of six from the multitude of busted, old, and mismatched plates. She put those in the cupboard, then set the others off to the side. She needed more boxes. Then she went to the cutlery and singled out one set for eight people. How was it Nan had ten different kinds of spoons here? Doreen stared at them in confusion and shook her head, then placed them with the odd dishes.

With the cutlery done, she started at the cooking utensils. But then she stopped and wondered if she was the right person to do this. All she'd ever used were the spatulas. There were two—one metal and one plastic. Deciding they were both decent, she put them back in the kitchen drawer and left the rest for Mack to help her sort. She really didn't know what else to use. So she instead went to the roasting pans and other dishes but didn't have a clue about which was what. Once again, all the pots and pans would be left for Mack to choose from. There were also bowls—multiple bowls, like mixing bowls, glass bowls, glass bowls with handles, and bowls with measuring marks on the side. She shook her head and muttered, "Good thing Mack's coming."

Just then her phone rang. "Hey," she said. "I was just talking about you."

"All good things, I hope," he said lightly.

"I'll need your help when you get here."

"Again?" he asked, his voice resigned.

"Easy stuff," she said. "I finally emptied the kitchen and scrubbed the room itself all down, but I've got everything kitchen-related in the living room, and I honestly don't know what a lot of this stuff is. There are so many different kinds of pots and pans and bowls, and I don't know why anybody would need all this stuff."

He chuckled. "That I can handle. I was checking in to see when you wanted to do dinner."

"A little later is fine. I just came back from a nice lunch with Nan."

"Good. I have some extra caseloads I have to work on. *Somebody* keeps dumping old cases on my desk." He sighed. "And, before we can close them, we have to check for other related incidences."

"You're welcome," Doreen said cheerfully. "Why don't you give me a shout before you're ready to leave?"

"I can do that." After that, he hung up.

Doreen went back to look at the rest of the canned goods. She shrugged. "Mack, you just signed up to help me sort all this mess." Turning, she returned to the kitchen to clean the dirty shelves and then put them beside the front hall closet.

Since that was settled, for now, she grinned and went over to Solomon's files. Grabbing Steve's big folder, she went out to the back porch, file in hand, and read. The journalist had worried Steve was money laundering. Doreen didn't understand how that worked because he was a lawyer, but then figured lawyers could be crooked. They probably had accountants in their pocket anyway. Well, at least her husband had.

And that reminded her of another lawyer—Mack's brother. She set out a notepad and started a to-do list. The kitchen and the living room went on the top of the list, while the two piles in the garage made it to second and third places. The closet followed after that. And then she added Mack's brother.

After that, she started a new page and jotted down notes about Steve. The journalist had handwritten notes summarizing Steve's life. It was all there—where and when he had graduated high school, where and when he had gone to college, where and when he'd gone to law school, and when he had passed his bar exam. She was fascinated as she read through it. Everything seemed nice and neat. She couldn't understand why the journalist had been so concerned with Steve.

When she got to the part where Steve was somewhere

around age thirty, she learned he had hooked up with a company called Brownwell. Apparently, there he became more of an enforcer-type lawyer than a corporate legal one. As in handing over payouts in return for silence. According to Solomon's handwritten notes, Steve paid off people to stop lawsuits. She wondered if that was considered normal legal work, then shrugged. It seemed like the world didn't operate in the same way she expected it to anymore.

Either way though, Doreen was happy studying the case files. She didn't have to take much in the way of notes because the journalist had done such a good job. It felt like working with a professional. Not to be caught without it, she got up and scanned in the summary. It would be nice if the journalist had put the files on a disk, but she didn't know if he had been computer-loving enough for that. Or maybe there were disks in the boxes she hadn't checked yet. She went through the Steve folders again, looking at the notes, interviews, and contracts. The contracts should have paid out immense amounts of money, yet somehow they were cut in half at the final payout signatures. She skimmed through the summary pages again. It was a fascinating read. But it wasn't very helpful in terms of understanding if Steve was a crook or not because, as far as she was concerned, all lawyers were crooks. Some of them played just inside the edge of the law. Still, she couldn't take her eyes off the pages.

By the time she finished going through the entire stack of files regarding Steve, the afternoon was almost gone, and evening loitered around the corner. Her phone buzzed, and Mack told her that he was on his way to her house and then promptly hung up.

She glared at her screen. "I'm pretty sure," she said, "I told you to tell me when you were leaving."

But a short browse through her phone proved he had, with a text, and she had missed it. She hopped to her feet and put on coffee, then carefully placed the Steve folders back into the box. As she did that though, she decided to scan the whole thing first. So, when Mack walked in her front door, she was still working on that project, with over two-thirds of the stack to go.

He looked at her, smiled, and said, "That's a heck of a pile in the living room."

She nodded. "It is, indeed."

He looked at the folder she held, and his eyebrows shot up. "Whose file is that?"

"Steve's," she said darkly.

He reached out his hand in an instant. "I want it."

"I know," she said, glaring at him. "And you can have it after I've scanned it. Possession is nine-tenths of the law, and it was given to me."

He shook his head. "In a criminal case," he said, "you don't have any rights." Something about his tone was gentle, but it was also fairly invincible.

"Pour us some coffee please."

He glared at her, and she shrugged. "I'm scanning these, in case somebody tries to steal them."

"In that case, make sure you send me the PDF too."

"You're welcome for Penny's file," she said, trying to keep his thoughts off of what she was doing.

"Right," he said. "I forgot about that. I should have hit Reply and said thanks."

"You should have. I'm not sure where all of it can be used, but I do know it'll help the defense. Maybe the prosecutor can use it to keep from getting caught with the information they didn't know about."

"Good thinking," Mack said when he returned with two cups of coffee and set them on the table. "How much more do you have to go?"

"Most of this, from here on in, is all on the same size of paper," she said as she filled the chute and hit the Scan button. "After this, I think it's just one more stack." She picked up her cup, then said, "Let's take a quick look through that stuff in the living room."

When they reached the living room, Mack just stood there and stared. "All of this came from the kitchen?" he asked.

"All of it. The cupboards have all been scrubbed down, waiting to be refilled." Then she grinned at him. "There's also the garage, which I have to show you afterward."

Too taken in by the mess before him, Doreen thought he barely registered what she had just said about the garage. He started sorting through the things. "It's always good to have tongs," Mack told her. Then he picked up another long-handled thing. "You need this for mashed potatoes." After that, he pointed at something. "And that's a slotted spoon for scooping up steamed veggies." Then he kept up his litany as he moved a pile off to one side and left a bunch in place. Finally, he said, "There. Most of the rest are broken and aren't of any value."

Doreen thought Mack was done commenting, but he pointed at the dishes. "Are you getting rid of those?"

She nodded. "I'm short on boxes again."

"I'm not surprised. You've taken so much stuff out of this place. You almost need a cardboard box factory to make it all happen." He added the utensils to the dishes and then started in on the bowls. "This one is a measuring cup. It's not a bowl, and there should hopefully be a couple more of them." He searched the pile, then spied something that interested him. He exclaimed, "Aha," and lifted three similar nesting cups with handles. He put those inside the bigger one. "You'll keep that set," he said as he placed them to the side with the utensils she was to keep.

After that, he sorted through the real bowls. "You need mixing bowls. These stainless steel ones will last forever, but these are pretty dented and look like they are scraped." Then he found brightly colored glass bowls. "Which do you like better?"

"The colored ones," she said.

Like a magician, out of the pile he pulled a set of four that nested inside each other. "Here," he said. "These are good ones to keep. Oh, and you might want to keep one of the big bowls too, just in case." He pulled out one of them and set it off to the side. Then he continued his inspection. "You've also got a wooden salad bowl set. And a glass set. Which one would you like for your salads?"

When she realized that was what they were for, she chose the wooden one. She put it off to the side, and he added salad bowls that went with it.

She laughed in delight. "I couldn't even see all these in there."

"Why don't you go put those away, and I'll get started on the baking dishes now?"

She hopped up and moved what he had sorted into the cupboards where she thought they would work well. She returned to witness him muttering to himself over the pots. He was checking their condition, mostly their bottoms, and whether or not they had lids that fit. Then he turned to her and said, "Put these away. They're good and solid. Nothing's loose or wonky. You have two good pots that don't have lids and a massive pot that's not necessarily a canning pot, but you could use it as one."

"What are those lids with holes in them for?"

He frowned, but his lips twitched.

She held a pointed finger at him. "Don't," she warned.

"Canning lids." He cleared his throat. Then in a very gentle voice, he said, "In the olden days, they tinned food. They put the food into tins, and it became 'canned food,' but nowadays we bottle them. You'll get canning jars and sealing lids, and you'll use a pot like that with the rack that fits it." He reached across and pulled out some tongs. "These tongs go with it too. Why don't you hang onto this? Maybe you'll want to make some canned fruit or fresh fruit purees."

Just the thought of that was enough to make her mouth water. She nodded eagerly.

He set the canning pot off to the side with all the related pieces that went with it. Then he returned to commenting, saying, "Roasting pans. Everybody needs one or two. I'm selecting two different sizes for you, and the rest can all go. They're either warped or bent."

Aside from the tin set, there was something else that had her curious. "What's that round ball thing?" she asked.

"It was all the rage for a while," he said. "You'd make these half-and-half cake pop things and insert a popsicle stick in it so the kids would have a little cake ball on the stick."

She just stared at him.

"Personally I like my cake in about six layers and slathered in icing, but to each his own." He shrugged, then set them off to the side. He picked up a weird bright red plastic thing. "These are silicone pans."

"How are you supposed to use those for anything? They'll wobble and drop for sure."

"I never really got the hang of it. Some people love them though." He shrugged again, then grabbed a bunch of cookie sheets, muffin tins, and bread pans. "You probably won't ever use any of these, but they're all in very good shape, and I don't want to shortchange you on the fun if you end up doing some baking."

She loved the way he put that. She smiled.

Then, with everything sorted out among the kitchen supplies, Doreen stopped to look at the scanner. She pulled the finished stack out, then started the new stack, only to land her gaze on a picture of Steve and Penny. The picture just sat on top of the stack of files she was supposed to scan. The two had their arms around each other. Doreen pulled the photo free and turned it over, reading the note on the back. And gasped.

*Stay away from Penny … she's my wife, not yours.*

# Chapter 11

*Friday Early Evening…*

"WHAT IS IT?" Mack asked from behind her, pouring a fresh cup of coffee.

"It's a warning note to Steve to stay away from Penny," Doreen said. She held it out for him.

"The scans may be problematic," he said, "since notes are on the back of some of these docs."

She frowned. "I thought I'd sorted everything that had stuff on the back but maybe not." She checked the rest of the stack. "Oh, that's the only one misplaced."

"Interesting," Mack said with a frown as he placed the picture on the kitchen table. "All it proves though is that Penny and Steve had a relationship."

"And she lied about it. And did George know?"

"No idea. But since it seemed like George had committed suicide, that may have been one of the many reasons why."

"I'd hate to think that George knew of his wife's infidelity. It's an awful feeling."

"And, of course, you know that firsthand. I'm sorry."

She nodded. "But it doesn't really matter anymore because that part of my life is over."

Mack tapped the notepad in front of her.

"Oh," Doreen said, remembering her list. "That reminds me. Have you talked to your brother yet?"

He shook his head. "We did talk a few days ago or maybe last week. I've been so busy that I haven't gotten an update from him on disbarring your divorce lawyer."

"Sorry," Doreen said. "I'm definitely responsible for a lot of the work coming your way."

"You are," he said with a chuckle. "But I'm not complaining. Crystal is coming home this weekend."

With her mind too full of Penny and Steve, it took Doreen a moment to remember who Crystal was. When she did, she cried out and raced to his side. "Really?"

"Yes," he said, grinning down at her. "The current plan has her flying in tomorrow morning."

"Good. I thought it would take much longer!"

"Well, the fact of the matter is, she's Canadian, so the embassy there in Mexico helped her get home right away."

"That's so soon."

"It is," he said. "While you're still scanning, let's go sort some more of the kitchen's things."

They returned to start with the canned food. He chuckled at seeing the potatoes, then set it off on one side.

"What we'll do," he said, "is separate everything that's over its due date. If it's under a year late, the food bank will take it. If it's over a year, it's for the garbage can."

Most of the food was past their dates. As they worked, Mack said, "We often see this in old people's homes. They forget that they've bought something, and they keep rebuying it." Then he chuckled. "This flour is quite old, and some of these things look rancid. I suggest we get some garbage bags and just toss out the bulk of this. When you do some baking, you can start fresh and buy small quantities."

The whole ordeal took them twenty minutes. And as soon as they got all the garbage bagged, Mack took it outside and dumped the bags into the trash can. He ignored the media that snapped his picture.

"Sorry," he said, when he returned to her. "But the media will think we're in a relationship or whatever."

She groaned. "They just never give up."

"They'll go away eventually," he said, looking around the kitchen. "Maybe you can find some bags to put the rest of these dishes and things in. At least they'll be packed up somewhat."

She did just that but then told him, "Now my cupboards are bare."

"Sure, but what you have is what you need," he said with a shrug. "And what's gone is stuff you didn't need anyway."

She beamed at him. "I like that." She walked over to the scanner and set the last group of pages to start scanning. Then she stood guard over the files and eyed Mack as he prepared the pork chops.

Without looking up, yet sensing she was looking at him, he asked, "Are you leaving Steve alone?"

She froze.

He frowned and turned to her. "I didn't mean to upset you, but I do want you to take this seriously."

She could see he was gearing up for a really good lecture, so, in a small voice, she said, "I forgot."

He narrowed his gaze. And his hands, covered with meat juices, almost went to his hips. He stopped himself at the last moment and walked to the sink, as if trying to hold on to his temper. He took his time washing his hands before turning around and leaning against the sink. Then he crossed his arms over his chest, and, in a very soft voice, he asked, "What did you forget?"

She wrinkled her nose. "I ran into him this morning."

"And you're just telling me now?"

"I did try to call you," she said in self-defense. "Honest. But I got your voicemail, so you were busy, and I figured maybe I'd given you more-than-enough work, and you didn't want to talk to me."

His eyebrows shot up.

She shrugged. "Besides, there wasn't much to tell."

"Let me be the judge of that," Mack said. "Tell me what happened."

She relayed a little bit of the event and tried to downplay it.

"And did you take it as a threat?"

She stared at him, wondering how she should answer, and then decided to be truthful. "Yes," she said gently. "I think I did."

"*Think?*"

She nodded. "Okay, so it was likely a threat. But he doesn't know what I know. He doesn't know I have these files. He doesn't know anything."

"But you did bring up the gun. He did acknowledge it was his, correct?"

She shrugged. "Well, he didn't say, 'Yes, it's my gun' or 'Yes, I dropped it when I flipped over the fence,' but he was shocked that I knew. And he didn't like the fact that I told him how you guys were coming after him."

"You really didn't tell him that, did you?"

"Well, I told him that he better have his answers straight before the police get to him."

"You realize, of course, he's probably halfway out of the country by now then?"

"Maybe not," she said cheerfully. "Honestly, I think he would stick around and make sure I didn't get to talk to anybody else instead. Plus, he's intent on telling everyone how I've made all this up about Penny."

# Chapter 12

*Friday Dinnertime ...*

THAT WAS A good way to end a conversation, and it wasn't a bad hook. But, in ways of getting Mack riled—well, Doreen probably couldn't have picked anything better. He slowly—ever-so-slowly—walked toward her.

"What did you just say?" His tone was low and ominous, but his glare burned with a dark fire.

She tried to backtrack and lighten the suddenly electric atmosphere. "Hey, I didn't mean it that way."

"There's no other way you could mean it," he stated. "Do you think you're in danger from this guy?"

She sank on a kitchen chair and seriously thought about it. "I don't think so. While I don't see him as the running kind, I'm not sure I see him as violent either. I think you guys were right in the sense that he's a paper pusher."

"Paper pushers can have hidden depths," Mack said in a hard tone. "Don't you dare go by that stereotypical assessment. He's a big man, and it wouldn't take much for him to overpower you if he wanted to."

"With a gun, he wouldn't even need to do that, would he?" Then she winced as she watched Mack's face bubble up with more rage. "Look. I don't think I'm in any danger," she said in a hurry. "I do need to go through his file though, to see if anything in there could particularly worry him."

"You already found that picture with him and Penny."

She just shrugged.

He didn't look reassured, but he went back to doing whatever he was doing with the pork chops.

"I'm missing my cooking lesson." She bounced off her chair and set her phone to video. "You're supposed to tell me what you're doing," she cried out. "You're not supposed to just cook for me. You're here to help me learn!"

"In order for that to happen," he said, some of his good humor returning, "you have to be here to watch."

"I'm watching now," she said. He reached for something, and she caught him wincing. "How is your shoulder? You took quite a blow getting run off the road."

"I didn't get run off the road," he corrected her patiently. "I know that's how you want to see it, but I did turn to avoid that."

"Sure, but I imagine the whiplash was terrible even if you hadn't avoided a direct hit. Shoulder injuries aren't so bad."

"Shoulder injuries aren't so great either," he said sourly.

She nodded. "I saw you wince."

At that, he glared at her; so she shrugged and subsided. Like all men, he hated having things he was trying to hide pointed out. He led her through the process of what he was doing, which seemed to be dipping the pork chops into the egg and then the grated parmesan cheese.

She sniffed the air. "It smells wonderful, and they're not even cooked," she said. "How does that work?"

"It's the richness of the ingredients." Swiftly, he placed

everything on a cookie sheet and into the oven to bake.

She continued to record as he brought out veggies, which he then made into a big salad. "I do love my salads," she murmured.

"Good thing, considering that's probably what you eat a lot of."

"I eat a lot of them because I like them," she said. When he was done, she said, "So there's still some stuff in that living room, but there's something even more important I need your help with."

He gave her a weary look but washed his hands and said, "Lead on."

She headed to the closet. "Remember this mess?"

He looked at it, nodded, then whistled. "Who knew this was such a deep closet?"

"Exactly. Anyway, I took out the shelves."

At the mention of shelves, he picked up the nearest one.

"No," she said. "What I need is that." She pointed to the ceiling inside the closet.

His eyebrows shot up. "But you're under the stairs here."

"I know, but boxes are up there, and I need them down here."

"Do you know what's in them?"

"No," she said. "I'm not tall enough even on a step stool to reach them."

On that note, he snagged a kitchen chair, put it inside the closet, and climbed up. "Looks like five or six boxes," he said. He shuffled toward the edge and carefully stepped down. It was a delicate retrieving process, and it took him six trips.

"This is an interesting little hidey-hole," he said afterward. "But it's pretty hard to access."

"Impossible for me," she said.

"Which also means impossible for your nan," he said, raising his eyebrows.

At that, both of them stared at the boxes. They were covered in dust, yet looked to be holding firm without any mice holes or droppings around them, but who knew what was in them? They were so covered in dust that she grabbed the vacuum, plugged it in, and vacuumed off their tops and sides.

When she was done, she asked, "Would you mind putting the shelves back up?"

While he did that, she put away her vacuum. Then, as if realizing something, Mack looked at the rest of the stuff on the living room floor, outside of the boxes and the kitchen stuff, and asked, "Did all that come out of this closet?"

She gave him a wry look. "All of it. And I haven't gone through any of it yet."

He shook his head. "Wow. But let's open the boxes and see what's in them first."

She walked over to the first one, flipped it open, and stared. White paper covered whatever items were in the box. She pulled out what looked to be very old china saucers and plates. "Dishes," Doreen announced.

"I wonder who from," Mack said as he reached into the box too. "Too bad this packing paper isn't newspaper so we could get a date."

"I know," she said. "I'm not sure if all these boxes hold dishes, but, once I open each one up, I'll take some pictures of it and see what it's worth."

Mack laughed. "You could have a nice set of dishes here."

"I could," she said. Just then she spied a piece of newspaper at the bottom. She worked the pieces up and out so she could unwrap another cup of the same set. They ignored it and spread the newspaper on the floor.

"It says 1896," Mack said with a whistle. "I didn't even know they had newsprint back then."

"They did obviously," she said. "But it certainly helps narrow down a possible date when these were packed." She stared at the boxes. "There's no identifying mark on any of them, and were cardboard boxes around back then?" He pulled out his phone and did a quick search. "Believe it or not, corrugated cardboard was invented in 1895, one year earlier. Wow. I did not know that," he said.

Doreen went to the kitchen, grabbed a paper towel, and rewrapped the cup that had been in the newsprint and replaced everything in the box. Then she went to the next box. It had more dishes. This time it was a plate that had the newsprint, which was of the same year. She shook her head. This looked like somebody's Sunday-best dishes.

On the third box, she opened it up and was surprised to find linens carefully packaged in some soft material. She pulled it out and whistled. "Wow, these are gorgeous."

Mack sat back and said, "Well, they look like linen to me. Pillowcases and sheets."

She nodded. "But they're hand-embroidered. And beautifully done." She looked at everything, then smiled. "You know something? I wonder if this wasn't the contents of a hope chest. Maybe somebody needed the actual chest itself and repacked everything into the boxes." She thought for a moment. "Did we get rid of a chest?"

"There was one with a rounded top and one with a flat top in the basement."

She nodded. "I'll have to ask Scott about that. I wonder

if any of them are back from this age."

"Doesn't mean they have to be. They could have been repacked multiple times," Mack said. Then he asked, "What do you mean by a hope chest?"

She gave him a beaming smile. "In the olden days—maybe not even all that long ago—it was a tradition. Young girls collected everything they would need for when they got married, and it was all kept in a big chest. Usually they were kept at the foot of their beds and were called hope chests. They included hand-embroidered tablecloths, bed linens, and dishes—things like that—so, when she moved from her parents' home to the home of her husband, she would have what she needed."

He nodded thoughtfully. "I could see something like that going on here. You've got dishes and linens here."

"Along with that, there should be cutlery and anything else she might have wanted or saved that was special."

They went to open the fourth box, and, sure enough, they found cutlery and more dishes. This time there were serving dishes and the utensils to go with it. When they got to the fifth box, Doreen couldn't help but squeal.

"These are all hand-stitched nighties!" She lifted one and held it up for him. It was long and made of the softest material she'd ever held, and it was simple, demure, and completely innocent looking.

"Can you imagine the young woman making these?" Doreen asked with a smile.

"I can," he said. "Of course, the husband'll rip that off her the first night."

Doreen shot him a look as he chuckled. "Let's not ruin the moment, shall we?"

His chuckle turned into a full and loud laugh. She ignored him and went through the other items. Indeed, they were all underclothes—from nightclothes to petticoats and garter belts and stockings.

"This is a fascinating inside look into somebody's life," Doreen whispered.

"Did you consider the fact it's all in storage and maybe that woman never got married?"

She sagged in place. "Wouldn't that be sad?"

"What else would be a reasonable explanation?"

"I don't know, but it would be fascinating to find out."

"Well, there you go. Another mystery to keep you busy for a while."

"You mean, keep me busy and out of your cases for a while. That's what you're hoping for."

His grin was slow to start, but it would surely split his face. He acknowledged it with a laugh. "Is that too much to ask?"

"No," she said as she pulled up the sixth box. "I wonder what's in this one."

When she opened it, she found it full of letters. She lifted a bundle tied up with red ribbon. "Oh," she said. "What's this?"

"I'm suspecting this is the correspondence with the eventual husband, and either it didn't happen because he found someone else, or maybe he passed on."

She opened the first one and smiled. "It's definitely a love letter from a Nadia to a Tom." She shook her head. "And yet, there are no last names."

"Any envelopes in there?" Mack asked.

Doreen looked in the box and said, "I'm sure there is, but the box is literally stuffed full with paperwork."

"That might be all you need to sort out your mystery,"

he said.

"I wonder if Nan knows anything about this."

"Good question. Maybe it's one of the things she bought in a case lot."

"Why put it up there though?" Doreen asked thoughtfully.

"That's for you to sort out," he said, getting to his feet. "As far as I'm concerned, it's dinnertime."

She looked up at him. "Already?"

"Already," he said. "Pork chops don't take long, particularly if they're baked. These weren't too thick either."

She followed him as she turned her video on again. Sure enough, the pork chops were golden brown and crispy. "Oh my," she said. "They look divine."

"Let's hope they taste that way." He stopped and looked at the kitchen table, then looked outside. "Where do you want to eat?"

"Outside, please," Doreen said as she dashed to the kitchen door and propped it open. Then she set the outside table while he served. She looked at the salad and the pork chops. "That doesn't look like it's enough for you though."

"I didn't cook any starch," he said with a shrug. "But then I had a really big lunch with the guys. Lots of pizza, so I'm totally okay to have rabbit food for dinner."

At that phrase, she chucked. "I eat rabbit food regularly. It hasn't hurt me yet."

"No, and neither has it slowed you down," he said with a mock sigh. "Wouldn't it be nice if it did?"

"Hey, you're grateful for all I do," she said. "Even though I'm probably a pain in the butt, and I make you endless amounts of paperwork."

"Yes, but I won't admit it."

"That's okay," she said with a grin. "I know the truth."

He rolled his eyes.

"So, what will we do about Steve?" Doreen asked.

Mack glared at her, then pointed back to the living room. "That's your cold case. It's got nothing to do with my cases."

She nodded. "You might want to question Penny about her relationship with Steve though. Although I believe it's a case of Steve wanting more but her heart was with George. George likely wasn't impressed if Steve tried to get too close."

"That's what the photo implies. Did you get me a copy of that by the way?"

"I will," she said. "I'm also sending you everything in Steve's file."

"Good, but just because he may have lost a gun in somebody's backyard doesn't mean he committed a crime."

"He entered my property with a gun in his hand, obviously intent on doing something criminal," she argued.

"And yet, you didn't report it to the police," Mack said, narrowing his gaze at her.

"I so did," she said, narrowing her gaze right back. "I told you."

# Chapter 13

*Friday Late Evening ...*

AFTER DINNER, THEY cleaned up. Then Doreen recovered all the papers from the scanner and stuck them in the folder.

Mack snagged the folder from her hand and said, "I made dinner, so you make coffee?"

She raised her eyebrows, thinking about it before speaking. "Fair deal."

She put on coffee but watched as Mack sat outside and went through the folder. He appeared to be locked into reading the journalist's summary first. Maybe he'd make better sense out of the corporate things mentioned there. But maybe not. She focused on the coffee.

When she returned, Mack intently read another set of summaries she hadn't seen. "Where'd you get those?"

"In the folder," he said, distracted.

She waited but realized there was no point. She might as well do the dishes. Not only had he cooked and showed her how to cook, but he had also done it multiple times now. So she did the dishes, and, when the coffee was ready, she brought two cups outside. He was still distracted. Now she wondered what she'd missed.

When he was done, he stared at her with a look she didn't recognize.

She frowned at him. "What's the matter?"

"Steve has been working for the Devil Riders," he said, his voice harsh. "And that is some seriously bad news."

"The biker gang? I heard they were a big group in this town."

"They're everywhere," Mack said. "And it was one thing for him to work with the legitimate business side, but it was another thing to work with the other side. It appears Steve, in his corporate legal side, deals with them almost exclusively. At least according to the notes."

"I didn't see that before," Doreen complained.

"You were so busy making a copy of it and being afraid I might steal it," he said, cracking a smile, "that you didn't get time to read it."

"True. So what does this mean?"

"It could mean Steve disappears—whether willingly or not—or, if he is afraid that something like this folder comes out, and he sticks around, he'll be facing bigger problems."

"Is this like a Mafia thing? Will the gang beat him up if this information gets out?"

"Yes," Mack said. "As much as they've tried to legitimatize the gang, there's still an offshoot where they believe they're above the law and can do what they want."

"Are they still into drugs, sex-trafficking, prostitution, and all that nasty stuff?"

He looked at her. "You come across the darnedest things."

"I've done a lot of research on these old cases recently. Of course, I've come across all kinds of fascinating tidbits. I also knew this biker gang was an element here, but it never occurred to me how bad they were."

"I'm not sure it's a bad gang in that sense, but Steve's been working with them for a long time. They may not even be currently involved in anything we're concerned about, but Steve may know of something from their past. And, if he's afraid you'll mess things up for him, that's a problem."

She shuddered. "Him being their lawyer doesn't mean he's doing anything illegal, right?"

"No, not at all, but, depending on how much research is in here," he said, "the journalist may very well have uncovered some illegal activities. According to his summary, he suggested the gang was laundering money through their corporations, while buying and selling properties all around the province."

"And so he's been using the corporation to help facilitate that?"

"Yes."

"And presumably," Doreen said, "they're laundering their own illegal money from drugs and prostitution?"

"Exactly." He handed her the summary she had not read yet.

She nodded and went through this summary, then put the pages inside, closed the folder, and shoved it toward him. "Then take him down," she said calmly. "And you're welcome."

He stared at her. "It's not that easy."

"I know. You'll tell me it's for a completely different department in the RCMP, won't you?"

His lips twitched. "We do all work together. But, yes, there are specialized crime divisions."

"So maybe don't handle this one all on your own," she

said. "Instead, hand it off to the right people."

"I would, except now you're threatening Steve with the police, and Steve has a lot of gang people he can call on to threaten you right back."

She stared at him. As she slowly sagged into her chair, she said, "Oh. Chances are the journalist uncovered all kinds of crap, didn't he?"

"Yes, but, if Solomon had any actual evidence pointing to a crime, he would have handed it to the police."

"Unless he was planning on writing a book and doing it that way?"

"No, he still would have given it to the police."

She didn't like the thought that came to her mind. She opened her mouth, then closed it.

Mack looked at her curiously. "It's not like you to hold back on your theories," he said. "Granted, you're not so free to share facts with me."

Just then Thaddeus hopped up onto the table, walked over, and pecked on the folder.

"Leave it alone," Doreen told the bird. "All kinds of nasty stuff are in there that once you open it …"

"Exactly what I would warn you about," Mack said. "If we continue our investigation this way, it could come back to the fact you are the one who had the folder."

"Which would put me out there as a target."

He stared at her for a long moment. "What were you going to say?"

She shook her head. "I've forgotten. I'm pretty sure it's more about Steve. And just being aware he could be dangerous."

Mack abruptly stood and put the folder on the kitchen counter. "I want to look at the rest of these folders."

She raced behind him. "You could ask first."

He shot her a look, and she raised her hands in surrender. "I've never held anything back from you."

At that, he spun on his heels and said, "What?"

She held her hands higher. "Well, okay. I don't hold anything back from you for very long."

He rolled his eyes and pulled out one of the pot chairs.

"Why don't we lay the folders down so all the names on the labels are visible, and we take pictures?" Doreen asked.

Mack nodded. "That's an excellent idea."

So that was what they did. They took all the folders out of one box, then arranged them to see all the tabs of names, without anything else to distract them, and took several pictures.

"I almost want to run all of this through the scanner so we have it saved in a digital format too," Mack said.

"I could do that, but it'll take me a couple days or so."

"I know, and I hate to even ask you because I'm worried about somebody getting into your house and stealing these now. But I'm afraid you'd be faster at this than going through normal channels at work."

"I know," Doreen said. "I could be sitting on a gold mine or a bomb likely to blast off in my face."

"Maybe I should talk to the journalist myself."

"You could try, but he's in a hospice. He had his great-nephew bring all these to me so it wouldn't be part of the estate. And I don't know if other family members know the great-nephew did this."

"Interesting. Makes sense to do this now before he dies," Mack said. "And then we may find out later that somebody's been waiting for Solomon to die to get their hands on this. I'll see if I get time, I might pass by. It's not a criminal manner to hand these off and he's not likely to pass any vital information that isn't in the file given his health."

"In that case," Doreen said, "I think I'll start scanning." While Mack put all the files back in the first box, she laid out all the folders from the second box and said, "Let's get all the labels down so we have photographs of what was here."

Later Doreen groaned when the photos of the files from the second box were finally done. "This alone takes a while," she said.

"Let's just keep the process moving," Mack said, then paused. "Why don't I finish up taking photos of the files from these last two boxes? For now though, while you run all that through the scanner, do you want me to take a look at the stack of stuff in the garage?"

She nodded. "I completely forgot about that. Tons of stuff is still there." She set up another folder with thankfully all normal-size papers into the scan tray and pushed the button before heading to the garage with him. He whistled when he saw the mound in the middle.

"You know what? I knew you were doing this," he said, "but I hadn't realized how big a job it would end up being. A lot of this is just garbage though."

"I agree, but I don't know how I'll get rid of it all. It's a lot to put out in the city garbage every week."

Mack moved a bunch of stuff around. "Some of this we can recycle. The others, we can probably take to charity. But old open bottles of shampoo? That's garbage."

"Exactly. And again I don't even know what I can recycle."

"Do you want to keep anything here?"

She shook her head. "Maybe you see things you think are valuable or useable that I'm just not seeing."

"We can start by separating what gets recycled and what's garbage. Then we can take another look."

Mack grabbed several bags and started tossing old shampoo bottles. Doreen smiled and headed back inside, setting the next stack of files to be scanned. Back and forth, back and forth—by the time they took a break, it was already eight o'clock.

Mack looked at the scanner and said, "I'm surprised it's not smoking by now."

"Don't say that," Doreen groaned. "I don't have the money to replace it."

"Did you work at my mother's place today?" Mack asked. "You normally go on Fridays, don't you?"

"Normally, yes." She nodded. "But your mom had appointments and asked me to come tomorrow. And I was too tired to do much of anything today besides this spring-cleaning effort."

He shook his head. "That's fine. I just didn't know if I owed you for gardening or not."

She wrinkled her nose. "No, but I'll do it tomorrow morning."

"I'm going over there to garden too, so, if you want, we can be there at the same time, and I can pay you at the end of it."

She brightened at that. "Perfect. Or I'll do the gardening for free if you can help me dispose of all this garbage."

"We'll see."

When Doreen came back from scanning the second box, she saw almost everything resting against the edge of the garage door. "So, was that all garbage?"

"I'd say so," Mack said with a nod. Then he pointed to a second pile equally as large. "We could do a charity run for those."

"Where?"

"There's a big one on Springfield. Other than that, various other places make money off your donations too."

Doreen smiled. "I can probably fit everything here into my car. If I knew where to go, I could just drop it all off."

"I suggest the place in Rutland. You just pull up, open your vehicle, and they unload it for you. You don't get any money though, but you get rid of what you're taking there."

She laughed. "You know what? I really like that idea."

So they opened the garage door and loaded her car. Doreen smiled when it was all inside.

"I wonder," she said, "if any of those plastic containers in our garbage pile could go to them. If so, I think we could get rid of a bunch more of this stuff."

They worked the garbage pile down by another one-third. With her car completely stuffed, and only a few trash bags left, Mack said, "Your garbage goes out on Monday. Then, if you fill it again after it's picked up, you can get rid of all these."

Doreen smiled and grabbed several bags. Together they filled her garbage can until the lid wouldn't shut. Now only one bag was left. She smiled and said, "That was pretty easy."

"Yeah. I'll take the last bag home." Then Mack picked it up and tossed it in front of the garage. "My can's empty."

"I have garbage I have to get out of the kitchen too. Maybe I'll give you a couple more bags, if you don't mind."

Mack ended up with three more bags, which would make it possible for Doreen to get rid of her garbage all by Monday. He had also loaded several boxes filled with trash in his truck bed, specifically for a dump run. "I'll take these to the dump. When you are sure you want to get rid of the spare bedroom bed, I'll take that later too. Just let me know."

Tired but euphoric, she smiled and opened her arms wide. "Thank you. I cannot believe we got that done!"

"I can't believe it either," Mack admitted. "You just have your living room floor to deal with now."

She groaned. "The closet contents. Right. But it's only the closet. My house is cleaned out of everything but a few pieces of furniture."

"Not even much of that. We may have to get you some used furniture."

"Maybe, but I don't know where to go for that either."

"Some secondhand furniture stores are around," Mack said. "I don't think that'll be a problem once you decide what you want. But live with what you've got for a while and see how you feel about it. Maybe you want to do some work on the house before you start filling it again with furniture. Even painting it would give the whole place a different look."

Doreen nodded. "You're right."

At that, Mack headed off. Doreen walked back inside, knowing she had done half the scanning, but another whole half awaited her. She also had a carload of stuff to get rid of, gardening at Millicent's tomorrow, and the front closet stuff to sort. She didn't know how her day had disappeared so fast, but it had.

She set the alarms, propped the kitchen chair up under the side door to the garage to stop anybody from coming in her house from that direction, and headed to bed. It had been another good day's work. But she was exhausted.

# Chapter 14

***Saturday Morning ...***

THE NEXT MORNING, Doreen woke up sore and tired again but almost euphoric this time at the amount of work she had accomplished. She also had a new mystery to work on. As she went downstairs, she remembered that she hadn't asked Nan about the boxes from the attic above the hall closet, and she still had the rest of the closet contents to go through. But it was also past eight, and she wanted to get Millicent's gardening done.

She stepped out into the garage and smiled. "Wow," she said. "Look at this. It's stunning!"

She wanted to open the garage door for the world to see, but did she really want the media to photograph her garage? Besides, she should cook breakfast and then do the gardening job she currently had because money still needed to come in to pay her bills. Now that she had paid a bunch of the bills, her bank account had taken a hit. But she'd deposited the cash for the car parts, so things were still good.

She whipped up an omelet, almost laughing at how easy it was to do, and remembered the one leftover pork chop from the previous night. She wondered if she could justify

"

eating it now but decided it was better to save it for lunch to go with a salad or something. So, seated with her plate and the animals sitting down to eat their food, she opened her laptop and browsed the internet for a few moments, looking for headline news.

Unable to help herself, she searched on Google for the biker gang named Devil Riders that had made its home in Kelowna. Outside of the fact they seemed to own a ton of property in the Knox mountain side of Kelowna, there wasn't much mention of them. At least not in the last ten or fifteen years. And that worked for her.

On that note, she searched Steve Albright's name, again in reference to the Devil Riders' biker gang too because that would be interesting to find out more about. She still wanted to get through all the rest of that material that Solomon had left with her. And she hadn't even started the scanning yet today on the last two boxes. Refusing to leave for Millicent's until she at least got a section done, she opened the third box and found they were all fairly thin files. She set herself a thirty-minute deadline and worked steadily. When the minutes were up, she only had four thicker folders left. She finished them within another fifteen minutes.

She still had to rename all these scanned files, but that would be a different problem. That would require another hour, which she didn't have the luxury of using right now for that purpose. She took the three already-scanned boxes and moved them into the office alcove area, where the scanner was. She stacked the fourth one still to be done on top. Then she opened the lid and realized these were much thicker folders and would take a longer time. Maybe tomorrow. Or maybe even when she got back this afternoon. She locked up her house, set the alarms, called the animals, and walked toward Millicent's corner.

As she walked into the backyard from the side gate, she interrupted Mack and his mother sitting on the porch. She waved at them and said, "Sorry. I hate to disturb you. I just wanted to get at the work early this morning."

Millicent was thrilled. She took her tea and walked to the edge of the porch. "So tell me. What's your new case all about?"

She heard Mack groan beside his mom. Doreen smirked and said, "Well, we found six boxes in Nan's attic from what looks like a hope chest from more than a century ago, but I haven't even asked Nan yet if she knows anything about it."

"A hope chest," Millicent said with awe. "That house of yours, it ended up being a treasure trove, hasn't it?"

"It's been fun," Doreen acknowledged. Then she bent down and got to work on the weeding.

Even just days since she'd weeded earlier, those pesky little buggers had popped up all over the place. She made a pile of weeds every so often and moved as fast and as efficiently as she could. Millicent kept talking with Doreen the whole time, wanting details of everything she'd found. When Doreen told her about the nightgowns, she looked up to see the older woman's face softening.

"I remember doing things like that," she said. "I hand-stitched my first nightgown for my wedding too."

Doreen laughed. "Good thing I didn't. I doubt it would have held together past the first night."

Just then she remembered Mack's words from earlier. She groaned, but, of course, Mack had already taken note of that and grinned at her like a madman. She glared at him, then went back to weeding.

"I told you that she was good," Millicent said to her son.

"Look at her move. How is she possibly that fast?"

Doreen didn't hear Mack's response, but it was likely not terribly nice. She had gotten him into a ton of trouble and had created a ton of extra work with her efficiency, so she could understand if he wasn't terribly thrilled.

When she finished making her way around to the rear garden, she still had about twenty minutes left. She grabbed a bucket and scooped up all the weeds she had piled up at various spots. Then she turned to Mack and his mom and said, "I'll move to the front and see how bad it is out there."

On the way she periodically stopped to pull up weeds that poked through the gravel along the sidewalk. When she reached her destination, she walked around the first garden bed. It looked pretty good, so she just grabbed a couple weeds, then headed to the second and the third beds.

The third garden had been skipped the previous week, and it looked a little worse for wear. Doreen grabbed her tools and dug up some of the weeds by their roots to slow the weeds from developing again, and, when her time here was up, she was pretty happy with the way it had gone.

She walked to the edge and dumped the weeds into the compost bin, then told Millicent, "You'll have to consider separating some of these plants or at least divide the roots and maybe come up with a way to keep the beds in check. I know the daylilies are looking mighty healthy, but, after they've flowered, you might want to spread them out."

"Oh, dear, I do. And the gladiolas! They've become such a mess."

Doreen laughed. "You know what? I always figured that's where they were happy. But, once they start growing higher, like they are now, we should probably cut and separate them off. Maybe you can make a new garden bed along the fence. You have that odd strip of grass there." She pointed it out. "I don't really see the point of it unless you want to keep it."

"Oh, I hate that strip," Millicent cried out. "That was my husband's doing. He thought it would be nice to have some walkway around the place, but honestly, it just ended up being hard to mow."

"So think about it," Doreen said as she motioned along the expansive fence. "We'd have to dig it out a bit and remove some of that turf, but you could certainly start splitting up a lot of the plants. I'm not sure what all else could use a bit of relief, but you can start with the daylilies and the gladiolas." And then she frowned and said, "As I recall, you had a lot of tulips. We could dig up some of those and put a nice soldier row of them along the front."

Millicent didn't respond, seeming to be in deep thought about it.

So Doreen said, "Just think about it. Nothing has to be done for a long time." Then she smiled and waved. "I'm heading home now."

Mack popped his head out. "How come you're in such a rush today?"

"Oh, you know," she said. "Things to do, files to read."

Mack called her phone as soon as she walked in her door. "You'll stay out of those files, right?" he asked in an ominous tone.

"I scanned the third box this morning," she said comfortably. "I want to get that fourth one scanned too."

There was silence at the other end before he grudgingly said, "Okay. That makes sense. Make sure you send me a digital copy of everything you've got."

"I will, but I have to rename everything, and that'll take

me a lot longer. I've got enough work for all of today just in doing that."

"Okay. Oh, and if you want to look for secondhand furniture, let me know."

"Will do," she said cheerfully. She set the scanner going while the coffee dripped. She studied the coffeepot, a little worried maybe she was getting addicted. She was only a little worried because, even if she was addicted, she wouldn't do anything about it. As she had found out too, since leaving her soon-to-be ex-husband, one joy in her life was having coffee outside in her garden. She wasn't about to give that up. She had lost a ton of stuff when leaving him, but that was one of those little comforts that she planned to keep.

As she walked into the living room, she frowned. Though she had moved the four boxes of Solomon's files out of here, still all the contents from the hall closet remained. She went to work sorting the multiple broom handles and brooms, then realized she should have gotten Mack's help with that too. There were wet mops, dry mops, and brooms.

With the big stuff handled, Doreen separated the cat food and the dog food, then contemplated where to put it all. No need for it to be in that closet, and it certainly didn't need to be in her living room. She went back to the kitchen, opened a bunch of empty cupboards, and found a spot she thought would work perfectly. Mugs's large bags of food went in the bottom, along with Goliath's cat food, while Thaddeus's birdseed went on the shelf above.

And, with that nicely secured, she returned and started in on the stack of paperwork in the front closet. The animals sat beside her, watching her more curiously, more likely than not attracted by the lingering smell of food that was no longer sprawled beside her. Thaddeus made a cozy spot for himself on top of the stack of papers, which wasn't helping, but Doreen scooched a large stack from underneath his feet. Recipes, recipes, recipes. She shook her head. "Nan, I didn't think you cooked that much."

Also, household tips and tricks for being a good wife. *Well, that could go in the garbage.* She crumpled up some paper into a ball and sent it flying across the living room floor. Goliath went from zero to sixty as he raced to whack it around farther into the dining room. She laughed at his antics. But Thaddeus didn't want to be left out. He eyed her, so she took another piece of useless paper, ripped it in half, made a smaller ball, and sent it flying for him.

That started an hour of playing catch and watching the animals scatter across the room. It wasn't helping her get any work done, but it certainly helped her mood.

She made it through the first stack, which was all garbage as far as she was concerned, but she did take the time to make sure nothing was important. When the Christie's people had been here, Doreen had found lots of valuable documents and then recipes too on the shelves in the pantry of her kitchen, so she wasn't sure why more recipes were in the front closet too. All the recipes should have been together. That made no sense to her. But then nobody said Nan was thinking all that clearly these days.

# Chapter 15

***Saturday Noon …***

B Y THE TIME Doreen had worked her way through half of the paperwork, she had to get another garbage bag to hold her growing mess. Maybe she could get Mack to take this crap with him, too, the next time he showed up here. It should be recycling though. She thought about it, then nodded. She still had quite a bit more to sort through though. So, determined to finally get to the bottom of it all, she grabbed another cup of coffee and sat down.

Her gaze kept going back to the boxes from the hope chest as she wondered about the letters. She had to unpack the dishes too and send Scott photos because, while she didn't know if it was financially or historically important, she did know these dishes meant a lot to somebody or had meant a lot to somebody. She still hadn't contacted Nan about it. On that note, she picked up her phone.

"There you are," Nan said. "I was deliberately waiting until you were done at Millicent's today before I called you."

"How did you know I didn't go to Millicent's yesterday?"

Nan chuckled. "My grapevine is invaluable. Besides, you

were bound and determined to get that house sorted, weren't you?"

"And I'm almost done," Doreen said. "I've got a couple stacks of paperwork from the hall closet that you had stuffed in the back of the shelves, intermingled with lots of bird-seed."

"Oh my," Nan said. "I can't even imagine what's all in there. They're likely nothing important."

"The first stack seems to have been recipes."

"You might as well ditch those. It's not like you're cooking."

"I'm getting better," Doreen said. "Of course, I still need more cooking lessons."

"How is that going, by the way?" Nan's tone was too casual to not be obvious.

"Mack showed me how to cook parmesan-coated pork chops last night."

"Oh my," Nan said in delight. "That sounds lovely."

"Plus, I had emptied your kitchen, and he helped me sort and get rid of about half of it. The last thing is this big pile from that front closet. Other than that, the entire house has been emptied out and scrubbed down top to bottom. It feels great."

Nan laughed. "Oh, I'm sad it's over with though."

"Me too in a way," Doreen said. "I've done almost all the clothing too. And I still have that bowl to sort through of all kinds of things stashed in the clothing."

"Like what?" Nan asked curiously.

"Like those little balls, like marbles, which were also in the Ming vase, and coins, bells, little bits of notepaper, some business cards—it was a mix."

"Ah, memories," Nan said. "Take your time going

through some of that stuff. I can't remember all that might be in there, but there could be something valuable."

"Speaking of which, I found a pair of earrings. I put them in the bowl, but I need to take another look at them."

"Earrings ..." Nan's voice turned thoughtful as she asked, "Do you remember what they look like?"

"Diamonds, I think, in a little heart shape, with a hanging teardrop."

Nan gasped. "Oh! I've been looking for those forever! Where were they?"

"In one of the twelve coats in the front closet," Doreen said. "I think I kept five of them, and I've got seven to go to Wendy." She frowned and realized those were still in the garage, but now her car was full of donations for the thrift store. "I completely forgot. I've got all those to drop off yet too."

"Lovely, lovely memories. Those are real diamonds, so make sure you take care of those earrings. They were a gift from an admirer."

Doreen rolled her eyes. "Nan, it sounds like you did very well off your admirers."

"It's not my fault if they were part of an era where men gave women gifts just because they were happy to be with them."

That stopped Doreen cold in her tracks. "That's a lovely way to put it," she said. "Too bad my husband didn't feel that way about me."

"Your husband was a drip," Nan said. "And that's about as nice as I can put it."

"I found something else though," Doreen said, thinking of the six hope chest boxes. "Remember how I told you about the trapdoor hatch thing I found? Inside the hall closet, in the attic, but underneath the stairs?"

With silence on the other end, Doreen could almost hear Nan's mind working as she sorted that out. "I'm not sure I do remember, at least I don't think I've ever seen it," Nan said thoughtfully. "In fact, I'm having trouble picturing it."

"That cubbyhole isn't actually in the attic because, of course, the second floor is above it. And it's not a big space, more of an alcove under the stairs. I don't really know how to explain it. You'd have to see it," Doreen said, studying the closet from where she sat. "But in that small space above it, I found six boxes."

"Oh, how lovely," Nan said. "I do love a good mystery."

"I do too," Doreen said with a chuckle. "The contents of all these boxes appear to be like the contents of a hope chest."

There was silence again. "A hope chest?" Nan asked, puzzled.

"Yes, several boxes are full of china. There are linens and nighties that look to be hand-stitched. They were very white and very virginal, so I presume they were for this woman's marriage. The last box is full of letters and paperwork that I haven't had a chance to get into yet, but the newspapers inside were dated in the 1800s."

Nan gasped, and then she cried with joy. "Oh, such fun. I mean, sad in a way because we'll never find the person who it all belonged to because she's no longer alive, but maybe some of her descendants are."

"So, you don't know anything about the boxes?" Doreen asked.

"No, not at all. I'd love to find out more though."

"When I get time," Doreen said, "I'll sort through the letters in the box. But first off, I'm finishing sorting through all the stuff in that closet, and then I'm scanning in the rest of all those files I got from Solomon's great-nephew."

"Right," Nan said. "That's very wise. We don't want to take a chance of anything happening to those files."

"No, we don't," Doreen said. "Do you know much about Steve?"

"Penny's friend Steve? That slimy lawyer guy?"

"I didn't realize you thought he was slimy but, yeah. I think we're talking about the same one."

"I don't know too much about him," Nan said eerily. "I like to deal with nice people."

Doreen laughed out loud. "How do you know he's not nice?"

"He's involved with that Penny person. You know she's a murderer," Nan scolded.

At that, Doreen sat back with a heavy sigh. "Yes, Nan, I do understand that. I just wondered if you knew anything about Steve's business dealings."

"Oh," Nan said. Something crafty entered into her voice. "You're hot on another case, aren't you?"

"No, not at all," Doreen said hurriedly. "But Solomon has a file on him, and Steve tossed his gun in the gardenia patch six houses down."

"And he's part of that biker gang, you know?" Nan added.

"I heard that," Doreen said. "I'm surprised you know that though."

"Everybody thinks I don't know anything, but they're wrong. I do hear lots. Besides, back then, Kelowna wasn't very big. It's certainly grown in the last twenty years though."

"But Mack said, just because Steve might have had

something to do with the Devil Riders' biker gang, doesn't make Steve a criminal," Doreen said parroting Mack's words which already mirrored her words.

"No, it doesn't. But making payoffs to people to keep them quiet, that's a different story."

Doreen straightened. "Do you happen to know anybody he did that for?"

"The Helmsmans, when their house burned down," Nan announced. "He gave Annette a payout. Although it wasn't much I don't think."

"Why did their house burn down, and why did he give her a payout?"

"I don't know. She's not talking. Because, when you take the gang's money, it's in exchange for silence."

Doreen winced. "Are you sure he wasn't just a lawyer for the insurance company?"

"Well, you see, that was the thing about the fire. There was no insurance on the property," Nan said. "They couldn't afford any. So that payout made all the difference in her life. Particularly as it was arson," Nan said. And then her voice changed, and she called out to somebody, "I'm coming. I'm coming! I've got to go, dear. I'm sure you'll have fun with those files. Keep me posted on that hope chest."

# Chapter 16

*Saturday Early Afternoon …*

"HELMSMAN HOUSE FIRE." Doreen quickly wrote down the little bits of notes she got from that conversation. Sometimes, with Nan, you had to grab the tidbits when they popped out. Otherwise, they'd be gone forever. Doreen might not be any better herself, as she was so scattered with so much going on too, sometimes. She had a hard time keeping track herself.

With the information on a notepad, she shifted, trying to scan the last box. She was grateful when it was all done because she still had to open all the PDFs and save them as the name of the related files. But as long as she had them scanned, they were preserved, and she could send a digital copy to Mack. She considered sending herself a copy of all the PDFs and thought maybe she should get a second email address just for secrecy.

It wasn't lost on her that she talked and thought like danger was around her. Probably for the best with her involvement in cold cases, usually involving murders.

But why would Steve pay out for a house fire? That was the thought that wouldn't let her go. Unable to stop herself, she got up, snatched her laptop, then sat down, and typed in "Helmsman arson house fire." Nothing came up. She sighed and realized the name Helmsman could be spelled a few ways so tried several different variations. But it still resulted in nothing. She knew she would have to send Mack a message, but, as soon as she did, he would know she was working Steve's case too, and then she would be in trouble again. It seemed like all she ever got into was trouble. Still, it would bug her until she knew more.

For her own sanity, she sent Mack a message, mentioning the Helmsman fire and arson, and left it at that.

Back in the living room, she dropped down again and went through more loose sheets of paper. And then she stopped cold because right in front of her were newspaper clippings. They were not related to anything that she knew about, but the top one read *Murdered*. Whistling softly, she made sure the papers she had just sorted had nothing to do with this and then carefully moved all the newspaper clippings off to one side.

And that was when she found all the rest—a good six inches of paperwork and newspaper clippings. It didn't mean they were all from the same case, but all these articles and documents would have to be looked through. Not having a clue what to do with it all, she sorted through them and made sure everything she had put aside to throw away so far was really garbage.

Then she got up and put the papers to discard into the recycling bin, so she couldn't mix up the stuff to keep with the stuff to toss. The recycling went out every second week, and it was due to go out this week, so that was perfect.

She came back inside and sat beside her stack of newspaper clippings, wondering what she could do to keep it all together because scanning these would likely be done manually, one by one. She went back to the garage, looking for a box or a bin or something for storage, and found one of the plastic bins she had planned to take to the thrift store. She pulled it out of the car, headed to the living room, and loaded all the newspaper clippings into it to keep them intact.

Then she walked back to the scanner and stood there until the contents from Solomon's fourth box was done. When she finally finished the last one, she closed the boxes and deliberately grabbed an old blanket and put it over the top of them, effectively hiding the fact they were file boxes. It probably wouldn't make any difference, but, as soon as she stacked other stuff on top of it, it would help it all to blend in. On that note, she grabbed a couple recipe books and tossed them on the top. She wanted it to look casual. Then she thought she'd ask Mack to store them in the secret area above the front hall closet the next time he was here.

In the meantime, she'd keep the physical files here, in case she had any questions about labeling one of the PDFs. Then she might move all four of these inside the hall closet, awaiting Mack to move them up into the attic.

Now in the living room, that left her with the six boxes from the hope chest and a plastic bin full of newspaper clippings. "Oh, Nan," she said. "What a crazy web we weave."

But then she stared at her wonderfully cleaned-up house and smiled. "Thank you very much, my dear," she whispered to the empty room. "You have given me a gift I have yet to fully reap, but I know it's immense. Thank you, thank you, thank you!" Then she snatched the box of letters, along with her bin of newspaper clippings, carried them to the kitchen, and put them on top of the case files.

She sat down with a cup of tea to relax a bit before starting this last scanning session. It would take much longer, since she was dealing with cut-out newspaper articles and would have to place each by hand on the machine. But she knew she would feel so much better getting this all scanned in. After she was done, instead of renaming each doc, she just copied all these individual PDFs into one folder and named it Newspaper Clippings found at Nan's House.

She couldn't wait to get into those too, but she was definitely tired. *Time to go to bed.*

# Chapter 17

*Sunday Morning ...*

DOREEN WOKE UP Sunday morning with a sense of satisfaction and well-being that she hadn't really had since she'd arrived. She looked around at her bedroom, clean, spartan, and somewhat organized. She could use a bigger dresser and maybe a few other little things on the walls to help brighten up and personalize her bedroom, but, for now, she was good with this, even with her mattress and box spring still on the floor. She was also thinking of getting rid of the old bed in the spare room. Cheerfully she got up and had a quick shower and then headed downstairs for her coffee.

Thaddeus hopped onto her shoulder from his perch as she walked past him in her bedroom, startling her. She reached up and murmured, "Good morning, big guy."

He rubbed against her head and said, "Good morning. Good morning."

She smiled in delight. "You're getting to be quite the talker, aren't you?"

"Thaddeus talker," he said, nodding his head. "Thaddeus talker."

She wasn't sure if she was teaching him stuff or if he was remembering his earlier education, but, either way, it was wonderful. Mugs raced down the stairs beside her. She found Goliath lying on the very bottom step, refusing to move. So hanging on to the railing, Doreen lightly hopped over him and said, "Nice try, Goliath. Tripping me up won't get your food any faster."

She put on the coffee before feeding the animals. Then, as that was done, she unlocked the back door and propped it open so she could see outside to the beautiful summerlike morning.

"It'll be a gorgeous day," she called out cheerfully.

The animals raced eagerly at her side as she headed to the creek with her first cup of java of the day. Even Thaddeus hopped from foot to foot beside her in excitement.

"I really need to put a bench here," she murmured. She wanted it on her property so she could sit here and not see anybody else while enjoying the view. The water made lovely little musical sounds as it drifted down toward the lake. It had risen somewhat, but it was still a long way from being anything more than a lovely babbling brook. Okay, so bigger than that but … At low water, the creek bed was wide, at least thirty feet across or maybe even twice that. She was really not good with distances. Still, the little bridge did quite well for that distance. She imagined that, at various times, the water probably rose up to the height of the little foot bridge, which just reminded her of that rotten slat of wood. She'd have to add it to her list of things to do— maintain that little bridge for her own peace of mind.

As she sat here, slowly waking up and enjoying the morning, she mentally worked on her to-do list. She should have brought a piece of paper and a pen with her. So instead, she pulled out her phone, opened a note, and started typing. She wanted to read those newspaper articles she had already scanned in last night, but she should probably ask Nan what they were all about first. She needed to rename the scans of the last of the Solomon files she had already done too, and that would be a couple hours of work.

She wasn't looking forward to that job. It wasn't hard by any means, but it would be tedious. And she also wanted to find a temporary place to keep the paper research files that was a little better than where they currently resided. At least until Mack came by to move them permanently into the attic. It had kept her awake last night because it was still obvious what they were. If she shoved them into the back of the front closet though, she thought they might just stack all on top of each other in the very back corner. The front hall closet was seriously deep. That would work for now.

More than that, she wanted to spend some time going over the box of notes and letters among the hope chest items she'd found in that cubbyhole above the closet. She knew that whoever wrote all those was long gone, but maybe some family members still cared. Or maybe they were long gone too. Nan didn't seem to know anything about it, and the house had been built in the 1940s. Doreen would have to check into whoever had built the house originally and those who had lived here before Nan. Could be they knew something about the hope chest boxes. Obviously, the house hadn't been built with those boxes sitting there, so somebody had put them up in the attic. She kept adding notes to her list, then added grocery shopping items on her to-do list as well.

She had left Millicent's so quickly yesterday that she hadn't really thought about doing the shopping afterward.

She wanted to make a trip to Wendy's too, but was the consignment shop open today? She wasn't sure when Wendy opened the store on weekends – if at all. However, the things already packed in her car were to be donated. So Doreen should take the load to that thrift store first in Rutland, then return home and reload her car and go to Wendy's. She wondered if the thrift shop was open. Pondering that, she headed back to the kitchen to get another cup of coffee.

It would be good to drop off all that stuff, empty her car, then go to a grocery store. Afterward, she could decide if she wanted to buy some furniture for the house or if she wanted to live with it empty for a while. That really appealed to her. And she also hadn't even had a chance to enjoy her work-shop garage. Plus, she hadn't moved her car *inside* the garage either. All those things, she planned on doing today.

With her second cup of coffee, she grabbed the bin of newspaper clippings and headed back to the creek. There, she sat on a big rock and slowly went through the articles. They spanned several decades. She frowned. Just then her phone rang. "Good morning, Nan," she said cheerfully.

"Wow, don't you sound happy," Nan said. "I gather you slept well."

"I did, indeed. And I got a lot more work done too."

"Great," Nan said. "What about the house? Is it all done now?"

"Not quite yet. I have those six boxes I have to find a place for because I don't know who they really belong to. Then I'll go through the one that's full of letters. Oh, and I found a stack full of newspaper clippings. I wanted to ask you about those."

"Newspaper clippings?" Nan asked thoughtfully. "Why would they be there?"

Doreen sighed. "I was hoping you'd tell me. There's a thick stack of them, Nan. Like four or maybe even six inches high. They're from like twenty-five years ago."

"I don't remember that at all," Nan said. "And that's one of the things I wanted to mention. I think a walk up your way might be a perfect way to get my morning exercise."

"Oh, that would be lovely," Doreen said. "Would you like to come for tea?"

"I just want to get out of here," Nan said. "I've been feeling a bit stifled since I woke up."

"I'm on the creek with a cup of coffee and the newspaper clippings. The clippings are one of the few things I didn't get rid of yesterday. Do you want me to meet you halfway and then walk back with you?"

"Oh, no, no," Nan said. "I'm perfectly capable of walking that distance. Just stay where you are. I'm already outside Rosemoor and at the creek. You should see me in a few minutes."

Mugs caught sight of Nan first. He barked several times and then bolted toward her. Doreen hopped to her feet and headed down the path toward her grandmother. She gave her a good morning hug, and the three of them wandered back slowly. Thaddeus still sat on the rock at the water's edge, and Goliath was stretched out on the path beside the plastic bin of clippings. Nan stopped to give both critters a loving. Thaddeus took advantage and hopped up onto her shoulder.

Nan sighed happily as she looked at the creek. "I should have taken out the rear fence years ago," she said. "This is really lovely. You do need a place to sit though."

"I know," Doreen said. "I was just thinking I should put a bench here so I can sit down and enjoy the view."

"Absolutely," Nan said. Then her gaze landed on the bin

of clippings. She shook her head. "Is this what you were talking about?"

Doreen handed it over to her. "Yes. Do you recognize any of these?"

Nan sat down on a rock and sorted through a couple of the articles on top. "You know what? I vaguely remember something about this, but I don't think I was collecting the articles."

"Meaning?" Doreen asked curiously.

"I think it was somebody staying with me. She was looking into something. Now if only I could remember what it was."

"I looked through it briefly," Doreen said. "But it doesn't seem to have any rhyme or reason."

"No, and that's quite true," Nan said with a frown as she flipped through more clippings. "It's a little confusing, isn't it?"

"It is. I'm not sure there's even a thread of continuity through all this. Maybe she was just interested in murder stories?"

"It's possible," Nan said. "But I really don't know. It makes no sense at all." She shook her head, placed the bin down, but then frowned as she looked at it again. She picked it back up and went to the very bottom of the stack where a clipping had a note tucked underneath. She pulled it out. "*Bob Small: Serial Killer at Large*," she read out loud. She lifted her gaze to Doreen. "Oh my."

Doreen was at her side. "What on earth?"

Nan handed her the scrap of paper and showed her where it had been tucked in. "I think you'll need to spend some time and go through this," Nan said. "Look at that. Another mystery and probably another cold case."

"If he's a serial killer," Doreen said, frowning, "it could be a lot of cold cases."

Nan beamed up at her. "I really love that you're here. You make things so much more exciting."

"Maybe, but all we could hope for now is that this guy is behind bars and already doing time for these cases."

"It's possible," Nan said, tapping the articles. "They're all older."

"I know," Doreen said. "I wonder who Bob Small is."

"You'll figure it out," Nan said. "I'm sure you noted some of these articles are from Vancouver. You know what? I'm pretty sure lots of serial killers were down there. If you think about it, it's the biggest of all the cities in British Columbia."

"I'll have to look into it," Doreen said.

"Yes, but I'm not sure when you'll have time between Steve and the gun and those boxes from a hope chest," Nan said. Then she looked up at her. "Any chance I can see them?"

"Of course," Doreen said. "Let's go inside, and I'll put on the teakettle."

Nan handed Doreen something she'd had in her pocket. "And this is for us to have with our tea."

Doreen chuckled. "Chocolate chip muffins, both wrapped together into a single packet. Did you steal them from breakfast this morning?"

"Can't be stealing if I already paid for it," Nan said cheerfully.

Doreen shrugged. She wasn't sure about the legality of such a thing, but she was happy to have a chocolate chip muffin anyway. Although she didn't understand how things like muffins, which used to be healthy and full of things like bran and raisins and molasses, became chocolate chip versions, which, to her, were more cupcakes. But it was one more mystery in the world of the kitchen as far as she was concerned.

Calling the animals to them, they headed back into the house.

# Chapter 18

*Sunday Late Morning ...*

ONCE INSIDE AND seated at the kitchen table with the back door wide open for a breeze and the teakettle on, Doreen started with the bowl of goodies she'd collected from Nan's coats—including the earrings and the opal.

Nan smiled at the sight of them. "They are just as lovely today as they were when I was given them," she said with a tiny smile. "And, maybe down the road, you could have that opal set into a pendant for yourself."

"Maybe," Doreen said doubtfully. But she really didn't know what to do with it for now.

"Now what about those boxes?" Nan asked, once again showing that monetary things no longer mattered to her. She was much more interested in the mystery boxes.

Shifting the bowl of pocket contents off to the side, Doreen unloaded the box of love letters. Nan cried out in joy. "Oh my, nobody does this anymore, do they? It looks like herbs or maybe dried flowers are tucked in between some of the letters too."

Doreen smiled. "From a romantic period that's now a bygone era."

"Oh, a lot of romantic things still remain in this world," Nan said with a big smile. "But this is lovely to see."

A pile of paperwork was on the bottom. Doreen pulled that out and stacked them, then laid it all on the table. "That's what's in this last box," Doreen told Nan.

"And what about the other boxes?" Nan asked. "Before we start into this, maybe I could see some of the other things."

Doreen led Nan to the living room, where the remaining five hope chest boxes were, as Nan stopped to gaze around. "Oh my."

"Right?" Doreen said with a chuckle. "And the upstairs is almost as barren as this first floor. I imagine it looks a *little* different than when you lived here."

Nan's mouth was still open when they walked into the dining room and all the way around to the laundry, kitchen, and back through into the living room again. "I don't think I've ever seen it like this."

"Only when you moved in probably."

"No," Nan said. "The people before us had been renting. I think they moved out and left a bunch of furniture behind. We had a heck of a mess getting rid of that so we could get our stuff in."

"*We?*" Doreen asked delicately.

Nan sent her a saucy look. "Well, it's my house, but I haven't always lived here alone, you know."

Doreen rolled her eyes. "Do you know anything about the history of the house before you bought it?"

"There was something sad about it," Nan said, pondering. "But I don't remember the details."

"I'm wondering if the *sad about it* part is this person with the hope chest. Although it's from much earlier."

Doreen opened one of the boxes and unwrapped one of the tea sets.

Nan sat down beside her and held out a hand. Then she cradled the delicate china and whispered, "It's beautiful."

"I know. I'll have to unpack everything and take photos of it. I've never seen a pattern like that."

"Neither have I," Nan said. "It's quite unique."

Doreen carefully opened something from every one of the boxes, and Nan shook her head.

"This is definitely from a long time ago," Nan said. "I wonder if it's a granddaughter or a great-granddaughter that hung onto it. Maybe thinking she could use some of it for herself."

"Or it was a family member that didn't quite know what to do with it and shoved it all up in the closet so they didn't have to be bothered," Doreen said.

"Where did you find it all?"

When Nan got up to her feet, Doreen walked to the closet where the birdseed had been sitting all that time and pointed to the in the ceiling up above.

Nan stared at it, nonplussed. "I don't think I ever saw that hatch before."

"All six boxes came out of there," Doreen said. "But nothing else was there. I had Mack take a look."

"Mack again, huh?" Nan asked in a cheeky voice.

"Yes, he's been very helpful," Doreen said firmly. Just then the teakettle whistled. "Let me go make the tea." Privately she thought it was such perfect timing. The last thing she wanted was to get into a discussion about Mack with Nan. It was liable to lead to more than Doreen wanted to discuss.

Tea made, they returned to the kitchen table and sat

there. Nan undid one of the bundled letters and read through them all. "These are early on," she said. "Undying confessions of love and plans for the future." She tied them again and went to the next set. "These are similar," she announced. "More thoughts of missing each other, some love declarations, and plans to get married."

"And the last ones?" Doreen asked as she brought the teapot over and settled two cups on the table.

Nan picked them up and said, "Oh, dear."

"Did he ditch her?" Doreen asked sarcastically.

"No. He got very ill. And his last letter said his time was done, and he wanted her to move on."

Doreen sat down at the kitchen table with a hard *thump*. "Oh, crap. That's very sad."

"They had some time to visit together," Nan said, "but he traveled a lot."

"And, of course, my mind immediately wonders if he was traveling or if he had another family or if he used that as an excuse to get out of something untenable."

"Oh my," Nan said. "You really have to change that attitude. Life is so full of good things. You can't be bitter for too long. It'll stain the rest of your view of the world."

"I'm not really bitter," Doreen said, "but I'm starting to understand more about evil human nature through these cold cases. Plus, everybody lies. That seems to be the bottom line—everybody has secrets, and everybody lies if it's convenient. Or maybe they finally tell their secrets when compelled to release them from their soul."

"I hope you're wrong," Nan said as she rebundled the love letters. Then she pointed to another stack of papers and asked, "What have you found there?"

"Well," Doreen said, "it tells me about a group of people. A family tree too and a birth certificate from way back and a marriage certificate and sheets from a Bible from the looks of it."

"That was quite common. They often kept a record of the births and deaths in a Bible. Marriages too. Of course, there weren't divorces back then."

"I know," Doreen said. She flicked through some of the papers, but they were faded and old. "It'll be hard to read some of these." When she got a little farther down, she stopped and said, "A death certificate." She pulled it out and nodded. "He did pass away. According to the marriage certificate, they were married."

"How sad," Nan said.

"Ah," Doreen said, tapping the papers. "There's also a birth certificate and a handwritten note about the birth of her daughter, Veronica. The date of the letter is 1901." Doreen paused, then said, "So she did have a surviving family."

"And chances are that woman is no longer alive either," Nan said, "because that's well over a hundred years ago."

"Exactly. Is there no mention in the letters that you read about a daughter?"

Nan shook her head. "But she may have found herself pregnant at the end of their correspondence by letters too. There was one visit where he had to leave again. During that time he was gone, he got sick."

"So, we take the date of that letter and add nine months," Doreen said. "We'd be looking for grandchildren or great-grandchildren now. I'll have to go to the library and see if I can find any records." She went through the rest of the papers and shook her head. "Some of this looks like it's been hand-copied, and some of it is just faded, but at least we have a date to work from. And I need her last name."

"The death certificate?" Nan asked.

Doreen went to the death certificate and nodded. "Phillips. Tom Phillips."

"So now you're looking for Veronica Phillips."

"Do you know who you bought the house from?"

Nan shook her head. "You should still have a bunch of those documents though."

Afraid that she'd missed something, she lifted her head, studied Nan, and then nodded. "You mean, all those folders I found."

"Yes. There will be formal documents in some of them."

"Good," Doreen said. "I can take a look at that then. I should probably organize those too. I just put them on the bookshelf in the front closet. I was so busy spring-cleaning everything else and thought I was done, but I'm not, am I?" She frowned, twisting in her seat to look toward the printer. There were still four bundles of folders and paperwork too. "I'll have to go through those myself."

"And you should," Nan said, "because who knows what you might find? It could be more receipts for Scott too."

"And he would like anything and everything we can find," Doreen said.

"What will you do with the dishes?" Nan asked.

Doreen shrugged. "I have no clue. I guess essentially I'll offer them to the family, if they're interested."

"Maybe if it was the first or second generation," Nan said, "but I highly doubt any of the subsequent generations will want them. Everybody is more interested in short-term now, not long-term."

"We'll see," Doreen said. "It's more of a curiosity than anything. After all this time, there might be a huge family, or there might be nobody."

"You'll figure it out," Nan said cheerfully. "I have the utmost faith in you."

# Chapter 19

***Sunday Early Afternoon ...***

BY THE TIME her grandmother left, Doreen was dying to delve into her research. Not only about the Steve issue with the Helmsman payout but also now a name and more paperwork to sort through on these six mystery hope chest boxes. And what to do with them was, indeed, a question that needed answers.

With her laptop and a sandwich beside her, as the muffin hadn't been enough hours ago, she sat at the kitchen table and forced herself to rename a certain number of scanned-in files before she did some more research. By the time she was done renaming and researching, hours had passed. She groaned and looked at the amount of notes she had taken. She would need Mack's help. That arson file was one of them. She texted him the name on the arson and the payout and said, "I think I mentioned this before, but I'm still looking for answers."

**That's nice** came his text in reply.

She cringed at that. Then she resumed her research. On a whim, she looked at the total number of Google pages of hits for this search, and it was one of ninety-seven. She clicked to load page twenty, then page forty, then page sixty, and stopped to take a look at each quickly. When she randomly went through a few more pages, a picture came up.

It was Steve, but a younger Steve with another woman at his side. The woman wasn't identified, and Doreen wondered how she could find out who it was. She saved it and read the article, which said he had been a benefactor to this woman who had suffered terribly in a house fire. Was that the arson payout she already knew about? She wondered about that and started delving into the different names that came up in the article.

That was the problem with research. When she found one rabbit hole, it led to a million other rabbit holes. By the time she was done, she had located three more house fires, all with Steve helping out. That really bothered her. She wrote those names down and texted them to Mack.

**Three new names re house fires and Steve handing over checks**, she texted. **Check into them, please.**

Just then her phone rang. "What are you doing?" Mack snapped. "First off, it's a weekend, and I'm not in my office. Second, why are you delving into Steve today, when we had this discussion already?"

"We did, indeed," she said cheerfully. "But, as I was doing this research, I came up with a bunch of other fire scenarios where he's handing over checks, and he's like this big benefactor. What if somebody he knows is lighting the fires? There's a problem or some purpose behind it, and Steve's out there, the good PR guy, getting all the kudos for being such a nice man, when in reality he's part of whatever is going on behind the scenes."

"Handing out checks?" Mack said. "But you can't tell me that is criminal."

"No, but *three* house fires?"

"Accidents?" he snapped back.

"One, yes. Two, possibly. But all three? Plus, the Helmsman fire is four. No," Doreen said. Then she mumbled, "That's okay. I'll just wait until I get all the evidence and present you with yet another case to put with your name and make it look like you're doing all the work." And she hung up.

She wasn't mad at him, just the opposite. This had become some game between them. But then, he really did have access to the information she didn't. She thought about Solomon's case files on Steve. Were any of those names involved in fires also mentioned in Steve's folder? That would be something. Would it be easier to search the PDFs? She wasn't sure. She opened his computer folder she had created and realized several PDFs for him were there. She searched each PDF for the four names. On the third PDF, something popped up. She read the article, and it was similar to what she had read earlier. She went to the physical folder, pulled out the paper copy, and flipped through it. There it was. Putting a paper clip on it, she set it off to one side and then kept researching the scanned-in PDFs and finding the paper documents in Solomon's folder.

Sitting down, she read the accumulated stack and interpreted Steve's actions as philanthropic, helping suffering people. But these dealt with just three fires, not the Helmsman fire. In the articles on these three house fire cases, the men had died, and the women had received money to help them out. Nan had stated Annette didn't have house insurance coverage. According to what she'd read in Solomon's files regarding the other three cases, there was no insurance coverage on any of the houses.

Doreen thought that was odd. Didn't anybody else wonder? This was a long time ago, so maybe Doreen would never know if the original investigators were curious about this too. However, if people were broke, paying for insurance might be one of the first things they couldn't do anymore.

She texted her findings to Mack. It would keep him on his toes and maybe keep her in his mind. Not that she wanted him thinking about her all the time. Right now, that would probably make him really angry. But she laughed and thought about the work she was doing and how it would benefit everybody. Buoyed with good humor, she started researching Steve as a philanthropist. And then as a corporate lawyer working for the Devil Riders' biker gang.

By the time she was done, she had a better idea of what was going on. The articles dealing with these three men who had died in the three fires were *all* part of a different gang, called *Satan Riders. Nothing suspicious about that.* She snorted in disgust. The women with children had all been given a check to help them move on without their partners. She thought about a rival gang who would take out a man and leave his woman and children alone, and then help them out. She wondered at that mentality. If these payouts had just left them financially well-off, that would have been nice. Of course though, Doreen had no way to know if the women received a big-enough check to do them any good. Or if the Devil Riders' biker gang had a hand in these men's deaths or the fires. No amounts were mentioned—and maybe it was a case of *Take this and disappear or else we're coming after you.*

Speaking of which, she realized she didn't even know where Steve lived, other than that he was a neighbor of hers. She searched for his address and found him in an article, standing with his arms around two other men who looked a little rough. They were in three-piece suits though and pretty nicely cleaned up. But she recognized that sharkish look about them. Her husband had the same look. She studied the photo for a long moment before writing down their names and Steve's address. And then she double-checked online to see if that came up as his address. Two other articles mentioned the street, so she assumed she was on the right track. But contacting Mack now was out of the question, or he'd be truly pissed.

Searching for the address, she found it a little ways away, on her side of the creek. And just across from Penny's place and up a couple houses. Which explained why Doreen kept coming in contact with Steve. Several large estate properties were up there. She was kind of jealous of that. He had three acres along the creek, and, according to the images she could see on Google, it was well protected and private.

Of course, he'd want privacy, wouldn't he? So how was it that he had a connection to Penny and to all these other women? She didn't think Penny had mentioned how they'd first met. Not that it was important but it was interesting. Doreen sat back and frowned. Did she get it all wrong with Penny? Did Steve have something to do with the murders in Penny's family? But, no, Penny had admitted to killing her brother, and Doreen knew George had admitted to killing her father and the nurse in his journals—not directly confessing on paper but enough to lead Doreen's imagination in that direction. Then George committed suicide, with the help of Penny and some lethal gardening plants.

So that took care of that. But that didn't mean Penny didn't know about other instances in Steve's life. How long had they known each other? Several decades at least. From that one photograph Doreen had found earlier, it was obvious they had a very close relationship.

She shook her head as she pondered this, then looked down at her critters, all stretched out on the floor, and asked, "Anybody want to go for a walk?"

Mugs went from zero to sixty once more. He jumped straight up in the air and then chased his tail in excitement. Goliath backed out of his reach and stared at him in disdain. Meanwhile, Thaddeus, who had been sleeping on his roost in the living room, flew toward her. He wandered around the corner of the hallway kitchen door, cocked his head at her, and said, "Thaddeus walk. Thaddeus walk."

She chuckled. "Maybe we'll take a coffee with us and a granola bar. We'll take a look at where our lovely corporate-lawyer-slash-scumbag lives. The fact that he's so close to me is a little disturbing. I would like to know where the enemy resides before he shows up here again."

Of course, Steve had already showed up more than a couple times. She brought a leash with her, just in case they had to be on the street or if they met some undesirables. She didn't want Mugs completely getting away. He was generally very good, but a little bit of caution never hurt.

Goliath, of course, had a mind of his own. Doreen was tempted to get a harness and put it on him but thought it would be more of a YouTube sensation to watch Goliath try to get out of it. Since she couldn't tether Thaddeus, she figured it wasn't fair to any of them. Tie up one and keep him a prisoner while the others were free? It was much better that they all learned to walk together. Which, she had to admit, they did. They were a very nice and tight-knit group most of the time. Hopefully, Thaddeus wouldn't get sidetracked, and Goliath wouldn't take off after him, and Mugs wouldn't decide something out there was worth chasing.

She could only hope that today, maybe of all days, they'd behave themselves.

# Chapter 20

***Sunday Late Afternoon ...***

THE WALK UP the creek was pleasant until Doreen got to where she always crossed over to Penny's side. And then she got melancholic and said, "Just think. If Penny hadn't attacked me," she said out loud, "or if she hadn't shot Hornby ..."

She was pretty sure the jury would let Penny off the hook on killing her brother on compassionate grounds alone, since she had been through a similar sort of abuse as her brother. But those recent attacks on Hornby and Doreen? Those were an entirely different thing. With her hands in her pockets, Doreen walked forward, past the stepping stones, wanting to cross over to see how Penny's garden looked but knowing she was here for an entirely different reason. She had never been up this far either.

She kept on walking as the creek lost some of its bank, making the traveling a little difficult. But, with the waters still low, she could walk along the creek bed itself. She just didn't want to end up falling and hurting her ankle and having to call for help. That would be humiliating. Some of the creek up here had really high banks, and she knew that some of them were private property, but along one side was a large pathway.

She should have crossed over when she could to remain on the safer path. Bridges, overpasses, and underpasses allowed for the walkway on one side. But, of course, she wasn't on that side. She kept on walking farther, recognizing some of the landmarks she'd seen on her Google search, and then finally she came to the corner where it looked like Steve's property started.

Immaculate lawns spread out in front of her. She could still continue to walk on the rocks and not touch his private property. As far as water rights went in Canada, you didn't own the water. There were the odd properties that had different rules written into ownership, but that would have been older archaic rules. Along here was a riparian zone, and you owned up to the high-water mark, but, once you got to a high-water mark, the city owned that and controlled what you could do with your land before it too. So she was allowed to walk where she was. It was Crown land. She kept going, only to realize Thaddeus had fallen behind. She walked back and offered him her shoulder. He hopped up, crooned against her, and tucked up along her neck. He was seated but staring up and around avidly.

"We've never been here before, have we?" she asked.

"It's new. It's new."

"It is, indeed, new," she said with a chuckle. Calling Goliath to her, they kept walking until they got to the end of Steve's property. It was a stunning location. It opened up to more farmland, horse pastures, and what looked like a big riding arena in the distance. Up and down, the path had disappeared somewhere along the line, but she figured that, from the looks of the worn path she was on now, this was an area people used when the water was low. She was probably allowed to walk along the grassy edge, but she didn't want him to see her.

It was certainly easy to see that big money had bought this property, unlike Nan's home, with its rough gardens and overgrown backyard. This place was so perfect she knew Steve had full-time gardeners and landscapers to make sure everything was tickety-boo. She knew it because it was exactly what she'd had before when married.

As soon as she passed his property, she climbed up the bank onto the real path and kept going. At least he wouldn't see her here. All she'd really learned was that he had a beautiful, expensive place and that he hadn't suffered by handing out money. But maybe if the biker gang realized Steve had something to say or that Doreen had something to say about his activities, that might change things.

She wandered down, hearing running footsteps behind her. She turned, wondering who it was. Then frowning, she slipped off to the side and took the stepping stones across to Penny's corner. If the water rose much more, she wouldn't get across easily. And, for Goliath, it would be traumatizing. She stopped midstream to look back to see him meowing at her. She returned, picked him up—and not even trying to stay dry—walked through the current to the other side. She just made it to the treed area on the other side, when she turned to see who was coming. A man ran past where she'd been. And, sure enough, it was Steve. She stood, frowning. Had he seen her at his property? And then she realized that, while she was here, he could be heading to her house.

On that note, she dashed back across the creek to her side, carrying Goliath, her heart racing with the realization she had once again not set the alarms and all that paperwork was there. She saw no sign of Steve anywhere. As she came around the corner, dashing up to her house, she wasn't sure if she was relieved or not. Until she got inside and made sure everything was still here and safe, she had no way to know.

She raced inside the kitchen door only to hear the door out front slam shut. Mugs barked, and she went through the house to the front door. There was no sign of anyone now. Of course. Where was the media busy taking photos when she needed them? She ran back to the kitchen door, worried he'd come around the side. But as she went around the side toward the garage, she saw somebody disappear over the fence.

She called out, "It's all digital!" At that, he tripped and missed a step but kept on going. "It's all right, Steve. I've already handed it all over too."

But he didn't stop. And she didn't know what else to do. She headed back into the kitchen. Sure enough, the physical folder with his name was gone. The clipped pieces she had removed from the file were still here, facedown, but not the folder itself. It was a good thing she'd scanned everything. But she'd wanted to keep all the paper copies too.

# Chapter 21

*Sunday Early Evening...*

DOREEN CALLED MACK.

As soon as he picked up, he said in exasperation, "I haven't had a chance to look up any of those names yet."

"Steve was just in my house," she snapped. "He stole his folder."

There was a short silence before Mack responded. "Did you catch him?"

"He jumped my neighbor's fence, but I did call out to him and told him that I had scanned it all. He damn-near fell on his face at that."

"Damn," he said. "Are you sure it was Steve?"

"He had on a black hoodie, but it was his body shape. I haven't checked if there are any footprints. I suppose I should have done that first," she said, reaching up to pinch the bridge of her nose. "That was foolish of me."

"Hang on. I'm coming over right now," Mack said. "Did you finish scanning all those files?"

"Yes, I did. And he didn't grab the things I had removed from his file, pages I had set off to the side. I was researching those this morning. They were upside down with paper clips on them. He just grabbed his folder and ran."

"But now he'll know what you know," Mack said. "And that could be bad news."

"Well, he won't know about the stuff I removed from his file. But maybe he'll wonder if there's more," Doreen said. "Because he found one folder, that doesn't mean it was the only one."

"You just have a nose for getting into trouble, don't you?"

"Are you already in the truck and driving over here? If you're not, I'm walking over to my neighbor's."

"I'm in the truck," he said. In the background, she heard an engine start up.

She smiled. "Good. I still have to get to that thrift store and empty my car."

"You haven't done that yet? You could have done that instead of getting into trouble," he snapped.

"And what if I'd been here when Steve came?"

More silence again.

She smiled triumphantly. "See? Maybe it's a good thing I wasn't here."

"Where were you? If you saw him leaving your house, where were you that you didn't see him enter?"

"I went for a walk up the creek," she announced.

"How far up the creek?" he asked suspiciously.

She frowned into the phone. "Just a little ways."

"How far up the creek?" he barked.

"Up to Steve's place," she said. And then added hurriedly, "But I didn't see him, until later as he ran by, and he didn't see me."

"It's a pretty damn big coincidence if he snuck into your house when you were at his. How is it you didn't see him?"

She explained what happened.

"That makes sense."

"Sure," she said. "That's when he almost fell because I told him how I had scanned everything."

"And that'll just have him coming back, wondering if you have a hard drive with it all."

"But surely he'll expect me to put it in cloud storage or to at least email it to myself. That's what anybody would do."

"Which means you're now a bigger threat than ever," Mack said morosely.

She was still talking when she heard Mack's truck. She stepped out the front door with the critters and waited until he pulled up in front of her door. She went to the big garage door and lifted it, realizing that once again, she hadn't locked that either. Mack hopped out and said, "What are you doing in there?"

She shook her head. "I realized I can now park in my garage. But you came here for something else." She walked over so she could see where Steve had jumped and pointed. "He went over the fence here."

"I wonder why he didn't go around the fence," he said looking around. "I see the reporters are gone."

"Of course they are, now that they'd be useful." She motioned at the fence. "This is only four feet tall. Someone like Steve, who's pretty tall, can jump this easily. I'm sure he didn't think anything of it."

"Maybe," Mack said. He walked over and up into the neighbor's lawn and checked the garden for footprints. "It's all bark mulch. No footprints to find here." He carried on across the front yard and over to the other side. Doreen hadn't met anybody in that house yet. Cindy and her kids were in the next house, but nobody came out when Mack wandered around that house's fences.

Mack shook his head when he came back and said, "No forensic evidence to show he was here."

"Of course not," Doreen said. "Just the fact that he was in my house. And …" She looked at him and frowned. "I don't think he was wearing gloves."

"You don't *think* he was wearing gloves," Mack said. "Or you *know* he wasn't wearing gloves?"

She cast her mind back, but it was hard to confirm. All she remembered was him wearing black. Her shoulders sagged, and she said, "He probably did have gloves on."

"Yes, he probably did," he said.

She led the way back into the kitchen and pointed to where the file had sat on the table.

"So, if he went into the kitchen and was looking around, it would have been right there, available for him, correct?" Mack asked.

She nodded. "It's a good thing I finished all that scanning." She picked up the pages that were flipped over and handed them to him. "These are the ones I found interesting in that folder. These are newspaper articles about the three different house fires and the women getting checks. These three men were part of an opposing gang."

Frowning, Mack grabbed the papers from her. "Do I have copies of this stuff?"

"Yes, in the digital file I sent to you. Although the file was big, so it's one of those Google link things you have to click to download."

He nodded. "I'll make sure I download it. But run me a paper copy of these too, will you?"

She took off the paper clips, went to her printer, and

made copies. With the copies clipped together, she handed them to Mack and said, "These are the ones I think are important. For all I know, there's more too because there's no mention of the Helmsman fire here. So that's another case."

Mack nodded. "I'll start on it Monday when I go in."

"Good," Doreen said. "I'm sure I can stay alive until then." She waved her hand airily at him.

At that, he fisted his hands on his hips and glared at her.

She smirked. "Also, I'm trying to find a Veronica Phillips. Her father passed away back in 1901, according to his death certificate. She apparently was the daughter of the lady who wrote these love letters and who owned the hope chest boxes."

"So, do you think they were married?"

"They were married just before he had to leave again," she said. "I'm not sure what his job was, but he got sick after he left. Then he died."

"But they still got married, so the hope chest was used?"

"I don't think she ever had time to get it unpacked," Doreen said. "Just time enough to get pregnant."

"Which we well know often happens on the wedding night if not before," Mack said quietly. "I don't know if I recognize that name. I'll have to take a look and see if I can find something on it."

"That would be good. A lot of names are flying around, and I've jotted down some notes, but it's a little confusing."

"You have a bunch of stuff you're dealing with too," he said. Then he caught sight of the plastic bin with the newspaper clippings. He frowned, picked them up, and said, "And what's all this about?"

"A friend of Nan's," she announced. "She collected all

these, and apparently, some of them deal with a serial killer from way back then—Bob Small."

His eyebrows shot up, and he turned to look at her. "What about him?"

She looked at him in interest. "So that's a name you know?"

He nodded. "He was a notorious serial killer in Vancouver many years ago. He was caught for a couple things and did time but was never caught for the murders. Only after DNA identification evolved was he linked to some colder cases."

"Does anybody know if he's still alive?"

"No idea," Mack said. "That's just one of the mysteries of the case."

"Of course," Doreen said. "Well, those I found in that closetful of paperwork."

"This house is just full of stuff to keep you busy, isn't it?" Mack asked. "Why don't you focus on that and leave Steve alone? You're prodding a dangerous tiger there. If he comes out of hiding, it'll be lethal."

"Maybe, but I'm definitely getting the impression it's not so much dangerous to me as maybe someone close by is dangerous to him."

"Explain."

"You already explained it," she said. "There's a chance somebody else knows this information is slowly being exposed. And they may stop Steve from talking."

"Just as likely they're afraid he'll let something loose," Mack said, absentmindedly flipping through the papers in his hands. "This is a big deal. You can't go playing around with this."

"Wasn't planning on it," Doreen said. "Steve wouldn't

matter to me in the least, except for that darn gun. If you would at least get the ballistics checked on it, we could see if it was used in any other cases. You'll get hurt … or worse … killed."

"*We*," he said with emphasis, "are waiting for ballistics to come back. I might hear by Monday or Tuesday but chances are good it will take longer."

"Perfect, because I've got a hunch it'll be a whole lot more than we expect."

"It shouldn't be. That would be foolish for Steve to use a gun directly linked to him or the gang or to several outstanding murder or B&E cases."

She snorted at that. "Did you ever know a smart criminal?"

He nodded. "Bob Small. That man was very smart if he did even half of what we're afraid he's done. He's eluded law enforcement for decades. We don't even know the scope of the crimes he's committed."

"How many killings are attributed to him?"

Mack shrugged. "He was a long-haul trucker. I don't think we'll ever know half of his victims. But, out of Vancouver alone, which was one of his main bases, we figured about thirty-two."

Her jaw dropped. "Thirty-two murders unsolved! How come the public doesn't know about this?"

"Because it was a long time ago. And I mean a *long* time ago. Law enforcement doesn't generally bring up things that far back. Not too many people are still left alive who even remember."

"But some are," she said. "And I'm sure many family members of those poor victims are involved too."

"Which is exactly why it popped up again," Mack said.

"Popped up again?" she asked curiously.

"Remember that we go through cold cases on a regular basis? Well, that one came up in discussion with the new genealogy cold cases."

"*Genealogy.*" She frowned. "Is that that new way of finding family members of somebody?"

"Yes, but it's a fairly new science. Of course, genealogy is old, and DNA is by now fairly commonplace, but to find the genealogy tree within the DNA ... That's an interesting prospect, and it certainly narrows down the field. That's where we got a hit on Bob Small."

She stared at him, then whispered, "That is an awful lot of cases."

"Too many," he said. "I'll handle Steve and Bob Small. You go find your Veronica."

She glared at him. "That's like telling the little woman to stay home, where she'll be safe and sound."

He leaned forward and said, "That's exactly what I'm telling you to do. Stay home where you'll be safe and stop getting into trouble."

"What you really mean is, stop interfering in what you consider your cases," she snapped.

He chuckled. "Exactly. If you decide to go into law enforcement, I can tell you the training is pretty rough. You might still be alive by the time you get through it all, but it'll probably drive you crazy because you don't get to work on any real cases for a long time."

She shook her head. "It sounds boring. I think I'll continue doing what I'm doing. These cold cases, a lot of them are so old they are public knowledge. I can dig as much as I want."

The smile wiped off his face. "You might, but you won't

survive every attack. You've been hurt enough as it is."

"I have," she said. "So I'll have to be smarter about it. I was hoping you'd be on my side," she said in a wheedling tone. "I have helped you a lot."

He just glared and said, "No blackmail."

"Of course not. I'll just see if I can get Nan's help."

"Oh, no. That needs to stop too."

"But a lot of people from Rosemoor have good information. Just look at all the boxes I got from Solomon. Do you know how much information is in there? Information that could have been lost if those boxes hadn't landed on my doorstep? Literally?"

He closed his eyes, and she could almost see his lips move, probably counting to ten. Finally, he opened his eyes again and said, "Bottom line is, you have to stay safe."

"Bottom line is, I've been safe so far. Everybody has come to my rescue. I won't expect it every time, but I can't walk away and turn my back on all these cases."

He glared at her, speechless.

She nodded. "So it's really in your best interest to help me. That way, I won't get into as much trouble, and we close these cases faster." Then she added in a smug tone, "And you won't have to worry about what I'm up to."

"I want you to take tomorrow off," he said quietly. "Monday completely off. Read a book, sit by the creek, … do something that isn't criminally related. Let Steve calm down too. Can you do that?"

She stared at him. "Why?"

"Because everyone needs to take a break. Even you. Step back. Relax. Clear your head. Tuesday you will think better and faster."

There was some sense to his words, but … she looked at

all the information she wanted to go through and opened her mouth to argue, but he placed a gentle hand on her arm. "Please. Just for tomorrow." Then he added, "Unless, of course, you can't handle that?"

Her head lifted, immediately geared up to accept that dare, that challenge, and she glared at him. "Of course I can."

"Good," he said. "I'll hold you to it."

Darn him anyway. … She was caught, and she knew it.

# Chapter 22

*Tuesday Morning Early ...*

THE MORNING DAWNED bright and clear. Doreen groaned with relief. She'd done it. She'd taken yesterday off completely. As per her agreement with Mack.

She still wasn't sure how he'd gotten her agreement, but he had. Now that torment was over. ... She had a bright cheerful grin on her face as she hopped out of bed with energy to spare. As she thought about it in the shower, she wondered if having the day off had helped. She'd taken the whole day to rest and to relax, forcing herself to ignore everything—at least as much as she could.

And she'd slept well and now felt wonderfully refreshed.

She groaned. But that would mean Mack was right.

Something she could never let him know ...

As it was, her day of rest allowed her to finally recover from the antiques, the gardening, and the heavy sorting and cleaning of her house. Although, as she realized from her most recent visit with Nan, she still had to go through the paperwork in those two bundles. Or four bundles. She mentally chastised herself for already trying to cut the work in half. But then she was grinning madly as she stepped out of the shower, dried off, and got dressed. It was all waiting for her … so, yay!

The animals were all waiting for her too. "So what do you guys think? What's on our plate today?"

Mugs woofed and jumped, then went to her, looking for a cuddle. Goliath stared at them in disdain. Thaddeus, on the other hand, wandered up and down the stairway railing, waiting for them to go downstairs. She led the way, only to have Goliath streak ahead and Mugs chase after him. She was chuckling by the time she hit the kitchen. She disarmed the security and opened the doors to the backyard. Everybody ran out except for her. She was more interested in getting coffee on first. Nothing like that very first cup of a day. Then, with the coffee dripping, she grabbed a pad of paper and a pencil and stepped onto the deck and sat down in the early morning sunshine.

It was already eight o'clock. Somehow her early morning had not been as early as she had originally thought. Keeping an eye on the animals wandering through the garden beds, sniffing out whatever critters might have come through the place during the night, she wrote down a to-do list.

She would get her car emptied today. She had gone through a few more of the clothes she had originally thought to keep and collected another full bag she would give to Wendy to sell on consignment, so she wanted to add that to the other bags going to Wendy already in her car. She also needed to get some more groceries. Mugs's dog food was looking a little sad.

With that thought, she hopped up to feed the animals. When they heard the bags shaking, they came running. She laughed and said, "You guys are fed now, but I'm not sure about me."

She opened the fridge to see a pretty dismal-looking selection. The leftover pork chop was long gone. While she looked inside, she realized she had enough for the always good old standby: a cheese omelet. And as much as she loved them, it was time to add a couple other foods to her morning repertoire. She could try scrambling the eggs but thought she'd end up with something either too liquid in form or overcooked. So it was an omelet once again. She poured herself her first cup of coffee and then made her omelet and took both out onto the deck.

A text came through from Mack. **How did yesterday go?**

**Perfect.**

**Did you rest and leave all the cases alone?**

**Yes. I hate to say it, but I'm feeling much more energized and alive today.**

That made her laugh. She was in such a benevolent mood, she realized she owed Mack more than she could ever thank him for, just for teaching her a few things. And that was besides learning she needed to take some downtime. She was a long way from doing much cooking, but adding even an omelet to her skillset had been huge. She really wanted spaghetti again, but the thought of making that sauce all on her own was daunting. She frowned, thinking about it. If she bought the ingredients, maybe this week Mack would stand by while she made it. She pulled out her phone and asked him.

When the text came back and with a solid block cap **YES**, she figured he was perfectly happy with that idea. And then wondered what she needed for ingredients. She walked back inside and picked up previous notes from her cooking lessons. And came back outside. She brought her laptop with her this time. She looked at her notes and saw she had most of it but wasn't sure if it was all. He'd gotten a little sneaky, adding in things, like wine, when she wasn't around.

She opened an email, copied over everything she thought went into the recipe and sent it off to him with a question about whether or not she needed anything else. She didn't expect to get an answer right away, since he should be at work, and she had certainly dumped enough work on his plate over the weekend. That reminded her of another stop she wanted to make. She frowned at that because she could take the animals with her to both Wendy's and the thrift store, but she couldn't take them to the grocery store or to the library. Not to mention the car was overstuffed.

And she really wanted to get some of this done. The animals appeared to be content on the back deck. Only now did she realize that taking down the rear fence meant she could no longer keep Mugs secured inside her yard. And Goliath—well, nothing would keep him or Thaddeus in. Mugs was generally quite happy to just stay in the backyard, but she didn't want somebody coming in and hurting him. She frowned and wondered what she was supposed to do. Taking the fence down had been a good idea, but she needed to put something else up. Or even just expand the deck and put a gate on it.

She loved that idea. She got up and wandered around, looking at the deck. It was pretty narrow and long, but there wasn't much grass growing on the left side of the house. So if she extended the deck enough for a table and maybe even a little barbecue, she could gate it by the steps and then Mugs couldn't wander the yard and creek whenever he wanted. She nodded to herself and wrote down another note about looking for plans. She figured that it would be cheaper to do it herself than to hire somebody. Still, it wouldn't necessarily be easy. She wasn't sure she was quite up for it yet. Something simpler first perhaps.

Still, she brightened. "I do have the tools," she said with a laugh.

But she put away that thought. After she was done eating, she put the animals back in the house, locked the door, set the security, and grabbed the last bag of clothes for Wendy, plus an armload of coats. She got into her car and headed out. Driving carefully past the few remaining media who flashed cameras in her face, she gave them a bright wave and drove off.

She started her errands by dropping off all the charity stuff first, delighted Mack was right when several young men did come out and unloaded the car for her. She was tempted to give them the bag and the coats for Wendy too, but then figured that, at least with Wendy's consignment, Doreen might get some money for those items. With that thought in mind, she headed to the consignment shop, parked outside the front door and walked in just as Wendy unlocked the door.

Wendy smiled at her, seeing the armload of coats and the single big black garbage bag, and said, "Are you finally getting to the end of it?"

Doreen nodded. "This is a bag of stuff I was thinking I would keep, but, as I tried them on, I didn't really like what it did for me. So there could be a few more of these because I did keep quite a bit on the first pass. And, of course, I brought the coats I don't want too."

"Let me grab them," Wendy said as they walked into the back. They hung the items on hangers. Wendy nodded. "These are excellent quality. I don't think I'll have any trouble selling them."

Delighted, Doreen said goodbye and drove to the library. She was planning to do the grocery store first but then thought that was foolish because everything would sit in the car while she was doing her research. Inside, she escaped the librarian's notice because she was busy dealing with other customers. She headed to the back to the computer and the microfiche film. She wasn't sure this was the best place, but, of course, Bob Small was somebody she wanted to get some older history on. And then she had those six boxes in her living room from the hope chest to research the even earlier years.

She rolled through the films as far back as she could, but Veronica wasn't showing up in the year Doreen was looking at. And there were hundreds of microfiche rolls, so she needed to narrow it down. Frowning, she couched that and started on Bob Small—there were tons from ten, twenty, even thirty years ago. She wondered if he was alive now. But nothing said definitively he was the serial killer, although he had been questioned several times. So he was a person of interest, but they never had any proof.

Which made him a very good serial killer, and she hated that she could even think that because why should anybody be a good killer? That was just so wrong. She sorted through Steve's articles online next, looking for the arson articles. And then realized they were too recent for the microfiches, and so she switched to the computers. She should be doing this at home really because then she could print stuff off for free. She hesitated and decided she was probably much better off doing this at home because these were public computers. Plus, for all she knew, the librarian could check the history of whatever she did when she was here. On that note, she cleared her cache, grabbed her notepad, and left the library, ignoring the librarian who called out to her.

She drove to the grocery store. That stop was much harder. By the time she had everything on her list for the spaghetti sauce, it looked suspiciously large and expensive. She had many of the ingredients at home, just not enough of some of them. She grabbed the regular things she needed, alongside the pet food, and frowned to see the bill would be a lot larger than normal. She still hadn't picked up any other meat. And she did need more. She grabbed cans of tuna and some cheese, then picked up deli meats for sandwiches.

She didn't have a clue on how Mack had done those pork chops either. So she walked past the pork chops and wondered just how hard it would be to cook a chicken breast. Not wanting to take the chance, she grabbed a rotisserie chicken and figured that would hold her for a couple days. The bill made her gulp, but she bravely pulled out her wallet and paid for it.

Inside though, she was shaky and worried that even trying to eat properly would wipe out her bank account. But then she remembered all the money she'd made off the car parts, the extra money Nan had given her for a dump run, and her recent bowl of money at home, and she knew she'd be okay for a while.

Back home, she unloaded everything, with Mugs more-than-slightly interested in the ground beef she had bought for the spaghetti sauce and the roast chicken as well. She gently moved him out of the way so she could get everything free and clear of him and where it all belonged.

She was almost done when her phone rang. She answered it, but nobody was on the other end. She frowned and looked at her screen to see it was an Unknown Caller.

She hated those. If people made a phone call, they should at least be honest about who they were when calling. She put down her phone and sat back to continue her research.

She should be going through the folders sitting off to the side, but her mind was stuck on Steve and those arson fires. By researching the individual names of the men who died in the fires, she found the same articles Solomon had printed off. But trying to find anything new wasn't fruitful.

Then, if Solomon was a good journalist, all this info would likely be in his notes and the rest of the file. Plus, the journalist had access to things she didn't have. She pulled up the PDF file on Steve from Solomon and sorted through a bunch of it. She was tempted to print the whole dang thing as the file was so large. Plus, it would be easier to read some of this stuff in print form. She looked down at it and saw it was seventy-seven pages long. She winced but decided to print off the notes at least. With that in hand, alongside a pen and her notepad, she did a timeline. The arson fires were all within two months—including the Helmsman fire.

*All in two months. Highly suspicious.*

According to what the journalist had noted, *Another gang was trying to move into town. The gangs were engaged in open warfare and had killed one gang member and had burned down his house. The Kelowna gang retaliated.* Three house fires and three other gang members killed made sense. Particularly if they were leaders whose deaths would have completely disbanded the rival gang and had the others in the gang either no longer involved or leaving town for better pastures.

"So four files." Doreen decided to add something to that note. *Four women paid off.*

But after reading that aloud, she sat back and wondered.

What would be the purpose of paying off the women? Did the Devil Riders feel guilty and did the women need this money? Or had the women helped kill the men or at least knew something about it?

It was all fascinating and confusing, but, as she read through Solomon's notes and articles, she found he had been extremely linear in his note-taking and had included damn-near everything she needed. So what was the motive behind those checks? It made Steve look like a philanthropist—a good guy—if the checks came from his own account. So what she and Mack needed to do was find out if Steve had been reimbursed for those checks. That made sense to her, if he acted as corporate counsel to the Devil Riders. But she wondered what was required for the police to get a warrant to check out Steve's financials.

She frowned, pondering the issue for a long time. She certainly didn't have that skill, and obviously, the journalist hadn't gotten that far. He likely couldn't get access. And what would it matter if Steve had handed over those checks? Outside of the fact he could be a lawyer for the gang or the insurance company, it didn't really mean Steve was involved in anything criminal, which was what Mack had said earlier. It was obvious to her that Steve was involved in something criminal, but how did one prove it?

Steve was too darn slippery. The fact he broke into her house and stole his own file was irritating too. The fact she told him all were scanned in meant he knew his attempt to steal all this information had failed. She wondered what his next move would be. If it was her, she would probably pack up and run because there was no way to stop the digital files from spreading. Once digital, it was always digital, and it could go anywhere. Particularly to the police. And cloud storage meant, even if he came back and stole her laptop, he couldn't remove all the copies she had.

Of course, that didn't mean he wouldn't try that though. Doreen opened an email and sent copies of the folders to herself and to her new special email she had created earlier and didn't share with anyone else. Steve wouldn't have the logins for that, so she could always access it. Now, who else could she send it to?

*Mack's brother, the lawyer.* She frowned at that because she didn't really want to start dumping additional work on him—not when she couldn't even pay for the work he was doing for her. But he could be a good additional holding place. Then she decided to avoid that contact for the moment. Better she leave it all with Mack instead.

Although Mack would need her to speak with his brother at some point, … she'd push it back a day, … a week, … a month or two. But knew she couldn't push it too far.

As she mused on what else to do with this information, she decided to put on a pot of tea. As she did, her mind wandered to Nan. She picked up the phone and called her.

"Good morning, dear," Nan's bright voice answered on the other end.

"Good morning, Nan," Doreen said with a chuckle. "Don't you sound fine this morning?"

"I am, indeed. It's a beautiful day. You've stirred up this place with new life. Now there's more gossip than ever. It's keeping me busy."

"Too much so," Doreen said. "It's obvious Steve's been working for the Devil Riders' gang for decades, but there's very little proof as to him having done any wrongdoing."

"There will always be proof. You must dig a little deeper."

"Right," she said. "I'm trying to locate the women who accepted the payouts to find out why they were given them. But then it's not like anybody is still in town. At least not according to my research."

"No, I wouldn't imagine so," Nan said. "If they were smart, they probably changed their names. Can you go down to the government office and find that information in public records?"

"I'm not sure," Doreen said thoughtfully. "But there must be a database somewhere, and there's probably a fee."

"Of course there is. The government will take money from you," Nan said. "I could ask around here if anyone might have known those women."

"Or the men," Doreen said. "The ones who died might have left a bigger impression."

"Oh, yes, I see what you mean," Nan said. "Deaths are more shocking. Really, does anybody consider the survivors?"

"Exactly," Doreen said. "You've got such a wealth of history at your fingertips down there at Rosemoor. I'm amazed."

"Well, just think about it. Solomon is still alive too."

"Good for him. I wish he'd had more evidence collected. He gathered lots of information, and it's obvious in his summary he thinks Steve is heavily involved in money laundering, but how does one prove that? Solomon didn't collect enough to take to the police himself, so not sure I can either."

"True," Nan said. "I don't think I'll have a chance to talk to him. I don't know."

"I hope you will. I certainly won't," Doreen said. "So, ask away, and see if anybody knows anything about it." Then before she hung up, she said, "Nan?"

"Yes, dear?"

"Be careful."

With that done, she put Steve's name on the new physical file folder and copied off the summary and her page of notes, then put it back into Solomon's file boxes. Between the four boxes of Solomon's case files and the six hope chest boxes, she was running out of room in that big front closet. She grabbed bundles of paperwork that Nan had kept on the shelves here, thinking they were by year, only to realize they were a complete jumble. She groaned, cleaned off the kitchen table and opened the smallest of the bundles. Then she sorted the receipts and the household maintenance documents, like insurance.

She stared at the insurance, shook her head, and whispered, "That's a half-million-dollar life insurance policy." She didn't even know if Nan was still paying for it. Good Lord. She set it off to the side and kept going. There were several receipts Scott would likely want, but she didn't even know if he had those pieces or not. She also had that stack of paperwork from Scott that she had just dumped on a shelf in the pantry. And that would be something else she had to organize and label in its own folder. Groaning, she realized, once again, that just when she thought she was done, she wasn't even close. Definitely needed to scan in those Christie's docs and save them somewhere safe.

# Chapter 23

*Tuesday Afternoon …*

I T WAS WELL past the lunch hour when Doreen sagged in her chair. She'd gone through all the jumbled bundles of Nan's paperwork, had organized those by years, and then each year was further broken down into Nan's different expenses. Doreen had massive stacks of that paperwork in front of her. She hadn't even gone through Scott's stack yet, the receipts for the antiques he took to sell at Christie's. But she had an empty file folder that she now labeled, where she placed all her Christie's paperwork so she didn't lose track of anything and so she had it all together.

Doreen scanned in the receipts and the like from Nan's records which Scott might be interested in. It was laborious as some of them had to be manually scanned, like the small original receipts. But, with that stack done, she put them into a separate folder and labeled it. Now, with two folders organized and labeled, she went through the other stacks. She figured one was garbage but wasn't sure. She'd have to ask Nan. All kinds of insurance forms had been filled out, but Doreen didn't know if they were completed or not. Some of them looked like evaluations for a rebuild on the house, and that just astonished her. Had Nan seriously looked at leveling this house and building a new one from scratch?

She didn't even know what that would entail. And, for a moment, she felt oddly protective of her home. After that, she set the paperwork she didn't understand off to one side and put a big clip on it. She might head to Nan's later this afternoon for a cup of tea and see if Nan had any answers. Another stack appeared to be legal documents, like insurance, deeds on the house, and some personal papers, like weddings and funerals. She clipped those together. Then she took the paper trash outside to the recycling can in the garage.

Now that she had all that done, and the scans of receipts sent off to Scott, she opened the folder she'd created for all the items Scott and his team had removed from her place. So many pieces were listed, including the artwork taken by Agatha and the books by John. She looked at the book list and remembered how John had taken damn-near every book she'd stacked up for him to consider.

She looked over at a bookshelf in the pantry and saw the four he hadn't taken. She wasn't even sure she wanted to keep them either. She brought them down, looked at them, and shrugged. She wrote down the titles, the authors, and the copyright dates to ask Nan about, and then reshelved the four books. Nan would say they were valuable, but John hadn't seemed to care. Doreen went through the rest of the Christie's folder to refresh her memory but then put it all away.

With everything tucked away except for the stuff for Nan to review, Doreen considered visiting her grandmother right away so she could get this mess off her plate. But she should probably call and let her know she was coming. Otherwise, Nan could be off doing something else.

Apparently, Nan was even lawn bowling these days. And that blew Doreen away. She'd yet to see the lawn bowling field, but it sounded like fun. One of the reasons she'd never really liked bowling much was the closed-in atmosphere and the loud noises. Not that Doreen had ever bowled. But she had attended a couple family-owned business events held at bowling lanes, clients of her then-husband.

She didn't understand that whole game; plus it had been very confusing with all the women in their high heels trying to walk on the bowling lanes. They weren't supposed to, and the staff had been beside themselves trying to keep these high rollers in check. But it also went along with the lifestyle she used to have. Just as she was figuring out what to do next and a little bit at odds with herself, Nan called.

"You should come for tea," Nan said.

"Why's that?"

Nan's voice lowered. "I have something for you."

"Did you talk to Solomon?"

"No, I can't get in to see him. It's something else."

Doreen jumped to her feet. "Well, I've got a couple things to ask you about too."

"Perfect," Nan said with pure satisfaction. "Make sure you bring the animals. I've got treats for them."

At that, she hung up, and Doreen chuckled. "Well, we've gotten a lot done today," she told her pets. "We might as well have a nice social visit. I really didn't want to do any more heavy work in the garden today anyway."

The fact of the matter was, she needed to work on her garden in a big way. One bed at a time for the moment wouldn't be a bad idea because she had to still get the weeds out. Then suddenly feeling guilty for having neglected her own space and her own plants, she rushed through her backyard with the animals in tow until her poor bedraggled yard was out of sight. She promised herself that tomorrow she'd get out in her yard and set up a plan.

On the way to Nan, Doreen reveled in the beautiful afternoon, and the walk was beyond enjoyable. She loved watching the creek as it slowly rose. The rocks were almost covered. She also pinpointed a few landmarks so she could gauge how much the water rose and how quickly it rose. She'd heard it could come on very fast, but she had yet to see it.

Meanwhile, Goliath was more interested in the ducks quacking alongside the creek. She could see his point. As she headed toward the turnoff, another series of ducks, much different in color, black with a little white on them, landed. Then they seemed to dive all the way into the water and come up somewhere else. She was fascinated and wanted to just sit and watch them and their antics but knew she was expected in a timely manner at Nan's. Finally, Doreen pulled the animals away and trekked onward. But, as she walked forward, she heard Goliath making a weird sound in the back of his throat, his tail twitching. He crouched against a rock.

When Doreen saw a duck with her babies floating up the creek, she gasped in horror, "Goliath, no!"

Goliath ignored her, his tail twitching and that weird noise continuing to come from deep in his throat. She didn't know what hunting cats looked like, but this was exactly what she imagined it would be. Not giving him any chance to argue, she picked him up and threw him over her free shoulder, Thaddeus riding on her other side. Then she scolded Goliath the whole way to Nan's. He didn't seem to argue. He just stared back, making more sounds from the back of his throat.

"We don't hunt baby ducks," she said for the last time. When she finally got around the corner, she thought maybe it was safe to place Goliath on the ground. He gave her a look, as if to say, *You don't hunt, but I do*. Then he sauntered forward, his tail straight up in the air, the tip flicking from side to side.

She figured there had to be a whole language of cat mannerisms. And, if there wasn't, she should start writing one. She laughed at that. She hadn't even had a cat for very long. The problem was, she was still trying to understand his language, and that was not exactly making life easy for her. She understood dogs much better.

She was still scolding Goliath as they approached Rosemoor to see Nan standing at the end of her patio, watching them with a big grin on her face. She bent over and called Mugs, who raced toward her, completely ignoring the stepping stones he was supposed to use. Goliath followed him in long leaps and bounces. That left Doreen and Thaddeus to bring up the rear. And, being properly respectful, she walked on the flagstones. As she got to the last one, she noted the gardener, standing there with a glare directed at her. She gave him a happy smile and a little wave. Then she hopped over to Nan's patio. Nan was cooing something unintelligible to both of the animals, who were lapping it up like they were suffering from a lack of attention for weeks.

"You know they're well-loved, right?" Doreen said in exasperation.

Nan chuckled. "I love to see them like this. You do bring such joy to my life."

Nan always said the sweetest things. Doreen reflected on how sad the missing years were when they hadn't connected like they should have. "I'm so glad I came here," she said impulsively.

Nan beamed. "Me too. Tea is already steeped. You took a little longer today, didn't you?"

"The ducks," Doreen exclaimed. "Goliath thought he should have one of the babies!"

Nan nodded sagely. "An animal is still an animal," she said, cocking her head and looking down at Goliath. He was stretched out in a patch of sunlight heating up a stone he'd claimed as his.

"I guess," Doreen said. "I just don't want him to be that kind of animal. He has lots to eat, no matter what he says."

Nan sliced something that looked delicious.

Doreen leaned forward and studied it. "Zucchini bread?"

"Walnut bread," Nan corrected.

"Ooh," Doreen said. "That looks lovely."

"It's from Mitzi."

Doreen froze with a fork on its way to her mouth. "Are you two friendly again?" she asked cautiously.

"Well, we might as well be," Nan said carelessly. "We've both been jilted."

It was all Doreen could do to smother her smile. "I'm sorry, Nan. Broken hearts are no small thing."

"No, they aren't," Nan said. "Of course, mine was never broken. And Mitzi's trying to be a little bit better."

Doreen chuckled. "Well, thank her for me. This is lovely."

"She sent it over for when you came by next. I'm not sure what you do, but everybody seems to love you."

"I don't know anybody who loves me," Doreen exclaimed. "People send me the oddest looks when I'm out and about."

"Of course they do. Those with secrets to hide," she said, wagging her finger at her, "know you're on the hunt for the next mystery."

Doreen rolled her eyes as she popped the walnut cake into her mouth. It was delicious with just a hint of cinnamon and a lovely accent of honey. She scarfed her piece, and Nan cut her a thicker one, then put it on her plate.

"Did you eat today?" Nan scolded.

"I had breakfast. A big one. But I didn't get lunch. I got involved in all that paperwork at home."

"Oh, good," Nan said. "I gather you brought some for me to look at too?"

"Yes," Doreen said. On that opening, she picked up the envelope she'd brought and pulled out the two clips full of papers. "A bunch of stuff is here. I didn't know if it's still viable or if I could just toss it." She handed the first bunch to Nan, who unclipped them and went through the documents, muttering away. By the time she was done separating this into two piles, she had identified less than twenty pages for Doreen to keep. All the rest went into Nan's recycling.

"Perfect," Doreen said. "And what's this about life insurance?"

"I've been paying it," she said. "It's one of those automatic withdrawal things. It's for you, you know."

Doreen stared at her. "You know you've given me so much, Nan."

"Well, you found out about the life insurance a while ago. We've just never really discussed the details."

"I know it came up," Doreen said. "But, when I found this, I wasn't sure if it was the same company or not."

Nan took the paper from Doreen's hand and shrugged. "You know what? I'll have to look into that. When you get home, send me a copy of it."

"Okay," Doreen said. "I'm not sure I have all the paperwork on any other insurance policies you may have to compare."

"Oh, that reminds me," Nan said. She hopped up and disappeared inside.

Taking the opportunity, Doreen ate her way through the second thick piece of cake. She wasn't sure if this classified as a bread or a cake. It was sweet enough to be a cake, but she hoped it had the health benefits of a bread. Not that she was worried about her weight any longer. That had been a constant in her life with her husband, but now that she'd lost so much weight, she was trying to put some meat back on her bones.

By the time she had eaten her second piece, Nan returned with another folder in her hand. "Would you mind making copies of all this too?"

Doreen took the folder, pulled out its contents, and saw they were Nan's personal documents. "Certainly. Do you want them digitized as well?"

Nan nodded. "That'd be perfect. You need a copy too."

Doreen placed it with her docs and said, "Now why don't you tell me what news you found out?"

"Hatty Hartley," she announced. "And Claude Hartley. They should be in the files. Or maybe in the police files. Mack should check."

Doreen sat back and looked at her. "What about them?"

"The sister of Georgia Monroe, Hatty, was killed—no, it was her husband, Claude, who was killed in one of those three arson fires."

"And do you—did you know them?"

Nan shook her head. "No, but Dick does."

Trying to keep all the names straight in her head, she asked, "Who's Dick?"

"He's one of the younger members here," Nan said. "Hatty was related to his niece, so he got the insider information on the fire."

"What did he have to say?"

"That it was murder. This Claude guy was dead, and the wife, Hatty, was given the money to keep quiet."

"That's what we figured," Doreen said. "But I didn't hear anything about him having been murdered."

"No, you have to go into the police files for that."

"Right," Doreen said. She snagged the pencil Nan had laid down, took out the notepad she had brought, and jotted down the names. "Okay, so we have one murdered husband. House gets burned, and the wife gets a check. Just like the other four cases, including the Helmsman case you told me about earlier."

"Yes, and Dick didn't say much else. It's just that the check went a long way to helping Hatty feel better."

"So do we know if Claude was a member of any gang?"

"Dick didn't say so, and I didn't think to ask."

"But did she help her husband to the grave is the question?"

Nan looked at her, and her jaw dropped. "Wow. I didn't think of that."

"But it's not like we can't consider it. She got a payout, and her husband and house disappeared."

"Yes, no family either."

"Any chance of asking her?"

"No, according to Dick, she took the money and ran.

He figured it was part of the agreement," Nan said.

The thing was, the deaths and the lack of witnesses were getting Doreen down. She clarified with Nan about the relationships. "If you can find out any more," she said, "I'm hoping to find somebody who was close to Hatty and who is still alive to ask about that payout."

"That'll be Dick. His niece is dead too."

Doreen sat back. "Wow. If I wasn't looking into this, and then Dick passed away, who would be left to even bring this up?"

"Nobody," Nan said simply. "That's why you can't do anything but dedicate your life to solving these issues."

"It's hardly a moneymaking venture though," Doreen said in exasperation.

"No, it isn't," Nan said brightly. "But once you get those antiques sold …"

Doreen stared at her in surprise. "I forgot about that." Nan laughed, while Doreen just sat there. "It doesn't seem real," Doreen said. "At least not until I get a check I can take to the bank."

"But it will," Nan said.

"Speaking of which," Doreen said, "John, the Christie's specialist, left four books behind."

Nan's smile turned to a frown. "He what?"

A little worried at Nan's complete switch when having her judgment questioned, Doreen pulled out the notepad. "These four."

Nan read Doreen's list and then laughed. "Okay, he's right. Those can go to charity."

"Oh, my goodness," Doreen said. "What a relief."

"I bought them from an old lady who thought they were important, and she was broke."

"So they were a goodwill purchase," Doreen said. She shook her head. "That was very sweet of you, Nan."

"I must have been in a generous mood that day," Nan announced.

Doreen, returning to the subject of Steve, said, "Steve isn't all that old, maybe fifty-something, so I don't know how involved he was in some of that gang-related stuff back then."

"Of course, he was younger then," Nan said. "Steve can't be more than sixty, and I think this must have happened a good thirty years ago. No, maybe not quite that long ago. Do you have any dates?"

"I have three, and they were all about twenty-two years ago," Doreen said, looking at her notes.

"That would put him in his late thirties, just when he'd be at his most arrogant," Nan said with a sigh. "But that doesn't mean he's guilty of criminal behavior."

"No, we need proof," Doreen said. "And, if the men were killed before the fire, the corpses would have shown trauma."

"Dick did say Claude was dead before the fire."

"Which means Hatty knew that." Exasperated, Doreen said, "It would be helpful to have more information from the family."

"I'll ask a couple other people about the other women," Nan said.

"Good enough."

Now armed with more information and paperwork and things to do, Doreen stood to get home. But, before she could move, Nan told her to wait as she ran inside. Then she came back out with a little ziplock baggie and cut two more slices of the nut bread.

"You can't give all of it to me," Doreen protested. "I'll get fat."

Nan shook her head and said, "You loved it. I saw you enjoy it."

Considering that, Doreen gave Nan a big hug and a kiss.

"Besides, with all the gardening work you're doing, you're not in any danger of gaining weight. Which is too bad. You're too skinny as it is."

"There's no end of gardening at home to do." Doreen frowned. "I'm so focused on spring-cleaning and organizing the house right now. Just as soon as I think I've got everything done, I realize there's another corner I have yet to turn over."

"Have you done anything in the garden?"

Doreen sat down with a heavy *thud*. "Not much. And I feel so guilty. I've been working so hard on all these cases and then doing Penny's gardening and Millicent's that I have neglected our garden. Mack made me take yesterday off and do nothing. Now I feel even guiltier. I should have been working on our garden."

"*Your* garden," Nan said firmly. "I don't want anything more to do with that. You'll have a hard time with parts of that overgrown mess."

"I thought, when I get back home, I'd take an hour or two and just work my way through it every day. Get a couple hours in daily. It might take me a few months, but at least that's progress. And then I could move things around as need be."

"I like that idea," Nan said. "You probably want a bigger deck too."

Doreen grinned. "I was just thinking of that this morning. I'll have to see how difficult it is to build a gate on the current one to keep Mugs in because I'm not spending the money on a contractor."

"Solomon's nephew who brought you all those boxes," Nan said, "his brother does a lot of that stuff."

"But he won't do it cheap enough for me," Doreen said.

"No, but a lot of it you can do yourself. Get his help to set up the structure and to get the foundation down, which he can probably do with big patio block things. But make sure you get it all lined up and leveled. If he helps you with that, you can do all the floorboards yourself."

"Oh, what a good idea," Doreen exclaimed. "I planned to pester Mack with questions on expanding the deck too."

"And you know that a lot of cops probably wouldn't mind helping you out for a day. Put out the word. Who knows? Maybe a few people wouldn't mind helping with the heavy lifting. Even some of your neighbors."

With that lovely thought in mind, Doreen collected her gang and headed home.

# Chapter 24

*Tuesday Late Afternoon …*

BACK AT HOME, Doreen filed away the papers Nan had asked her to keep, all in a separate folder with notes from today and such as Nan requested. Then Doreen ran these pages through the scanner and also copied the stack Nan had asked her to do. Finally, she renamed the digital file and emailed one to herself and one to Nan. With that done, she placed the copies she had to return to Nan on the table and filed hers away.

She was getting good at this. But she also needed a system for all this note-taking. She opened up a Word document on her laptop and typed some notes on Steve's case. Once that was done, she researched the Hartley family tree. The summary from the journalist on Steve's information had been a huge help to her, so Doreen wanted to continue with a summary of her own, writing down the information Nan had gleaned from Dick re this new name, the Hartleys. But that was a little more confusing. Still, Doreen did the best she could from her chicken-scratch notes. Didn't Nan say the husband had been murdered first, then burned in the house fire?

For that, she needed Mack. She dialed his number, and, when he answered, his voice was distracted.

"Hey," she said. "Have you got a moment to talk, or are you busy?"

He gave her an exasperated sigh. "I work full-time, you know."

She winced. "So, does that mean yes or no?"

"I've got a moment," he said. "Sorry. I just came out of a meeting. That always makes me frustrated."

"I can imagine," Doreen said, commiserating. "Meetings are more about people sitting around in a circle, avoiding the work they really have to do at their desk."

At that, Mack let out a bark of laughter. "For somebody who never worked a corporate or government job in her life, you seem to have a good idea of how meetings go."

"You can blame my ex for that," she said bluntly. "He used to always complain about the fact that meetings were useless, and nobody ever did anything they were supposed to do."

Mack was still chuckling when he asked, "So, what's the problem?"

"The arson cases. There's a fifth one, but I don't have a file on that one yet. I just heard in a roundabout way from Hatty Hartley that her husband, Claude, was dead before the fire. Did your records show that?"

"I haven't had a chance to pull those cases yet," he said. "I thought you were leaving those alone."

"Dick, at the retirement home, had a niece who was re-lated to Hatty in some way," Doreen said, confused how that worked herself. "But Dick said Hatty got a payout to keep quiet. Remember how we were trying to figure out why the women would have been given a check? It wasn't out of the goodness of Steve's heart. It was to keep quiet. Because the husband had been murdered first, and then the fire was used to cover up the murder."

"But forensics should have shown if he was killed first."

"Maybe, but what if it's a soft-tissue wound?"

"Usually, if there's a body, they go through the remains of the fire very carefully," he said. "The autopsy would show if he was alive before he died from the fire."

"Sure. But let's think about this. If he's shot in his bed on the second floor, and then the fire ravages the house, so basically nothing is left—just a few bones. That bullet would have either gone through the body or would have been burned in the fire. The body wouldn't even be on the second floor anymore, depending on how fierce a fire it was, so the bullet is somewhere in the remains of the carcass of the burned house. Are you really telling me they'll find it?"

"I would hope so, yes."

"*Huh*," she said in confusion, thinking about finding a bullet in the ashes. "Well, could you check the records to see if this is new information or that maybe you guys already knew Claude was murdered first?"

"Besides, for a fire to burn that hot, you need an accelerant."

She noted how he had sidestepped her question. "Of course," she said. "Hence, you guys already know it was an arson case?"

*Silence.*

She smirked. "I'd love to hear back on this when you get a moment," she said and hung up.

It was already late in the day, and she hadn't done any gardening because she'd been so busy doing paperwork, but that was no excuse. Before she ate, she was determined to get something done outside. She hopped to her feet and, instead of her usual tea, she grabbed a bottle and filled it with cold water. Then she grabbed her gardening gloves and opened the back door, letting everybody out into the yard with her. "Let's go get some physical work done," she said.

She'd already done work on the echinacea bed, so she chose the next bed to work on. As she looked toward the house, she was determined to work on a couple feet of her garden every day. With that thought in mind, she stabbed her shovel into the ground to mark what she should get done today and started pulling weeds. One hour later, she hit her mark. She crowed in delight. "It's not that bad after all," she said to Goliath.

He was lying on his back, his four legs in the air, snoring. She laughed, pulled her phone from her pocket, and took a picture. Then she sent it to Mack and Nan. She captioned it A Hard Day's Work, then put away her phone. After that, she kept on working for another hour, determined to get a little more done. By the time she got another section done, she realized she hadn't expected near enough from herself. She could do a lot more out here. Within a month, she could have this whipped into shape and at least know what the devil was planted here. But it was enough for today.

She stepped onto the deck, wiping the sweat off her brow, and looked with pride at the six feet of garden she'd cleaned up.

"That looks good," Mack said from behind her.

She let out a shriek and turned around, glaring at him, her shovel already in defense mode. He took a step back, his hands up, but his grin said he wasn't sorry at all. She still glared at him. "I have been attacked too many times in my own home and in my own yard. A little warning would be nice."

"A little warning definitely," he said. He crouched to hug Mugs, who gave him a great big welcome. Even Goliath walked over and flicked his tail at him, looking for some cuddles.

Thaddeus, on the other hand, was still perched on a branch of one of the maple trees nearby. He looked at Mack. "Thaddeus is here. Thaddeus is here."

Mack chuckled and walked over to give him a hug. Well, it was more like a stroke on his breast. Thaddeus hopped on Mack's shoulder. "He doesn't really wait for an invitation, does he?" Mack asked.

"No," Doreen said cheerfully. "He does what he wants, just like the rest of them."

"Well, that's fair," he said. "Seeing as how you do too."

She glared at him again, and he cracked a smile. Then he said, "There was no evidence that the Hartley man killed in the fire was murdered."

She gasped, and her face lit up. "Perfect. So, that's new information."

"It's a new supposition," Mack corrected. "Remember that thing called *evidence*?"

"If you didn't find a bullet, they killed him in another way. And, like you said, an accelerant was used, so the fire would have burned hotter than normal." Then she paused before saying, "What I want to know is where were the women at the time of each of these arsons?"

"I checked, and apparently Hatty was out for several hours that evening with girlfriends, and her alibi checked out."

"I wonder if she knew the money was coming," Doreen said, a cynical tone to her voice.

"If that was the case, that would make it premeditated," Mack said.

"She's dead now, so there's not a whole lot you can do about her. But we need to find out if the other arson cases are similar."

"The other three, which were the opposing gang fires, I did check. And, yes, all three men were burned in the fires with no evidence they were killed beforehand."

"There had to be a reason why they didn't get out of the house fire," she said. "And don't tell me in all cases the women weren't home."

Mack shoved his hands in his pockets and glared at her. "Yes, that's correct. But their alibis were very different. One wasn't even in town, visiting her mother in Vernon, and the second one had a wedding to go to, and the other one was in Vancouver for the weekend."

"Oh, how very convenient," Doreen said sarcastically.

"Yes, there are notes to that effect in the file, but the fact remains that their alibis check out and that no evidence was found to link them to the deaths of their husbands."

"Of course not. The wives were told to get out of town and to stay away. Rather than be home and die with their men, the women took off. That's love for you."

He shook his head. "You've got to work on that attitude."

She wrinkled her nose. "Sorry, it's still a hangover from my ex-husband."

"With good reason," Mack admitted, "but you can't let it completely destroy your attitude."

"No, it won't. Eventually," she said. "So, how do we find out if these men were dead first?"

"Well, there were no lungs to check to see if any smoke

was inhaled," he said. "Their bodies were pretty well incinerated, and that was done deliberately on the part of the arsonist."

"Sure. So we'll assume they were murdered. Otherwise, why go to those lengths?"

"And again, no forensics."

"No, but the link is Steve."

Mack crossed his arms. "Just because he handed over a check …"

"But did the check come from his own bank account? And, if it did, was there a corresponding deposit to his bank account from the Devil Riders? Either someone gave him the money to hand out or someone reimbursed him for that payout money."

"I might take a look at that." Mack studied her for a long moment. "I still need a legal standing to get into his financials."

"It's there. We just have to keep digging. And I know you weren't on these cases originally, so are the original investigating officers still around to talk to? The journalist made it very clear those payouts were for something, and that Steve was behind it all."

"Too bad the journalist didn't come up with any proof he could bring to us, so we could have done something about it then or now."

"I know," she said. "He's still alive though. Not in very good shape. He's on his last few breaths apparently, in a hospice. But Nan thought she might stop by and see him."

"I could also drop by, if there was a potential legal reason, but I don't want to upset a dying man."

"Agreed. So we have to do more research on Steve."

"The cops have been looking at Steve for a while," Mack

said. "But again, we're lacking evidence and real viable reasons to go any further into his life."

"I don't like the legal system sometimes," Doreen announced.

Mack laughed. "Most cops don't either, but we're sworn to operate within the law. And that means there are limits to what we can do."

"He entered my house illegally. Why don't you do something about that?"

"Can you prove it was Steve? You know attorneys. They'll twist your words inside out and backward and say it could have been anybody and not him at all."

"I know," Doreen said morosely. Then she was quiet as she thought about her options.

"What are you thinking about?" he asked suspiciously.

She beamed. "I was thinking of a trap."

Mack shook his head. "No, that won't work. Steve's been operating like this for a long time."

"Sure, but that doesn't mean his gang will like it. To hear that the file was unearthed. What if I just happened to let people know this file is full of all kinds of incriminating evidence and names?"

"Which is why Steve stole the folder in the first place," he reminded her. "To ensure that information doesn't get out."

"But people don't know that, do they? And they certainly don't know if there are more files that he didn't steal."

"You're asking to have your house burned down around your ears," he warned. "Have you forgotten that's the way these gang people get rid of problems?"

That stopped her. She stood here for a moment, arms crossed over her chest. "Well, we have to do something. This is hardly acceptable."

"Agreed. Let me think about it, okay? And I want to read up on the arson files. Did you get anywhere on any of the other harmless stuff? Like the woman who had the hope chest?"

Doreen shook her head. "Not yet. Nan doesn't know anything about the boxes found in the attic, and I just photocopied some paperwork for her on her house and stuff. And I completely forgot to look at the deed of trust on the house to see who Nan bought this house from. I'll do that when I go back inside."

"Good," he said. "Remember. Focus on that first."

"I will. But I'll hardly forget the Bob Small stuff either."

At that, Mack spun on his heels and glared at her.

She raised both hands in frustration. "I know serial killers are dangerous. But honestly, I think Steve is one of the most dangerous. He operates in the shadows, like a snake. And he lets people get away with all kinds of shit. It shouldn't be allowed."

"And we're on it," Mack reminded her.

"Yes," she said, grinning. "*We're* on it."

# Chapter 25

*Tuesday Early Evening ...*

AS SOON AS Mack left, Doreen picked up a cup of tea, walked to the creek, and sat on her rock. She understood Mack was worried about her, and she needed to be careful, but what was she supposed to do when obviously somebody was heavily involved with now five house fires, all arsons and likely all murders? The first house fire—the Helmsmans—probably started it all. And that was also arson. Doreen had no idea how far this went or how big it was.

And the other problem was how many of the original gang members were even still alive, whether of the Devil Riders' gang or the rival gang? How many were left to be prosecuted?

She understood there was Steve, and he shouldn't be allowed to walk away scot-free. He had a good twenty to thirty years left to live, even if fifty or sixty years old now. Why should he be allowed to enjoy his freedom when he'd caused so much suffering and pain and loss?

Of course, it didn't matter what she thought. So much was going on around her that had nothing to do with her. But then she remembered Mack's words about how Steve, or the Devil Riders' gang, could burn down her house in retaliation for all her research and interest into this matter. She hated to say it, but one of her first thoughts had been, *at least the antiques were safe.* She also had to wonder about the house insurance and if it was up to date. She mentally noted to check on that, making sure she added fire if it wasn't already covered. Although she thought it was mandatory. But she hadn't paid insurance bills before.

She groaned. She had so much to learn about owning a home, particularly for somebody who'd never even paid her own cell phone bill before. And how did the insurance work if her house burned to the ground? Was it still insured if the damage was caused by arson?

As she sat here, she realized that the Penny-and-Steve connection meant that Penny's defense would be a lot stronger if Doreen wasn't around to testify. On that note, Doreen worried that maybe her half-put-together security system wouldn't be enough. Her animals would need rescuing in the case of a fire. And Penny did have some money to pay for an arsonist. Particularly if she sold her house. Doreen didn't know if Steve would do a favor like that for free for somebody he obviously cared about, but it would also benefit him to not have Doreen around. And that was yet another consideration.

She stood and called Nan. "Do you have house insurance, like for a fire, on this place?" she asked as soon as Nan picked up.

"Of course my dear," Nan reassured her. And then her voice sharpened. "Why?"

"I was just sitting by the creek and wondering," Doreen said, glibly not dwelling on the reason for the call. "Just thought to myself I haven't paid a bill like that yet."

"I always pay annually. It'll come due in the fall," Nan said. "Hopefully, by then, you'll have the money from the antiques."

"I hope so," Doreen said. Then she worried about the cost. "How much does the insurance run?"

"It's about a thousand, I think," Nan said.

Doreen gasped. "That's a lot of money!"

"Yes," Nan said. "It is. You've also got to consider the property taxes too."

"And what kind of money is that?"

"Several thousand. You'll get that notice soon. It's always sent out in early July. You'll get a grant for being a home-owner, but it won't be quite enough to help offset the cost."

"Right." Doreen could see her bank account like a great big bathtub, and the plug pulled out, and her left with no money at all. "Those are some fairly major bills."

"They are," Nan said. "But I'm here, and we'll get this done."

"I hear you," she said. "I just wish you didn't have to worry about it. That I was doing well enough without your help."

"That's not today's issue," Nan said. "Did you find anything new on these cases?"

"No," Doreen said. "Nothing yet."

"What about Mack? Did he find anything?"

"No. He's looking into a bunch of stuff but nothing new yet."

"Okay," Nan said. "You'll let me know when you find something, right?"

"Yes," Doreen said. Then she hung up, looked down at the animals, and asked, "Do you guys want to go for a walk?"

Mugs's response was a crazy wave of barking and dancing around, whereas Goliath didn't even appear to open his eyes. Thaddeus sat here, sleeping on a rock, and he didn't appear to notice either. Frowning, Doreen reached over and gently brushed his feathers. "You not getting enough sleep, big guy?"

He shuffled away from her fingers as if she had disturbed him. She sighed and said, "Well, I'm not going without you unless you want me to take you back inside."

At that, he straightened in outrage, stretching up as tall as he could. "Thaddeus is here. Thaddeus is here."

She chuckled. "I know that, you big crazy guy," she said affectionately. She held out a hand, and he hopped on and then walked up to her shoulder, where he sagged close to her neck. She rubbed her head gently against him for a long moment and then told Mugs, "Okay, let's go."

As she walked away, not seeing Goliath though, she looked back. He still snoozed in the sun's light. "Goliath," she called out.

He opened his eyes and, seeing her leaving without him, jumped up and raced ahead.

She laughed. "I didn't think you'd want to be left behind."

They walked to the crossway to Penny's house. Doreen really wanted to take a look, despite not knowing if the house was even for sale anymore, what with Penny being charged with these crimes. But then realizing she was probably out on bail and that was a good-enough reason to keep away, Doreen kept on walking.

Really, it was Steve's place she wanted to go to anyway. It was a longer walk, and it was early evening now, with the sun just starting to dip. She'd missed dinner, and, somewhere along the line, she was worrying about the oncoming night. As she got to Steve's property, the late shadows of sunlight stretched across his land. She stood here for a long moment. It was a gorgeous place with a really lovely layout and a beautiful and fresh green garden. But it was paid for with blood money. And that was something she could never reconcile.

She walked past his property and up to the next one, wondering exactly what was here. She found out it was another big mansion, and she found nothing but mansions for the next ten or so properties, at least from what she could see. She kept walking before she turned around, then walked past Steve's place again. As she did, she thought she saw somebody in the windows. A curtain slammed closed. She frowned at that, lifted her phone, and took a photo. And then she hurried past and walked back to her place.

By the time she got in the door to her house, a deep sense of unease had settled inside her. And yet, she couldn't really justify or explain it. Something was not quite right. Instead of sitting out back, she made herself a hot lemon drink and sat out front. She didn't know why she chose the hot lemon. Somehow she was suddenly looking for something different to drink these days.

She sat here wondering what she was supposed to do now. She had so many open threads and no answers on several cases. Doreen hadn't found anything new on the Helmsman fire either. She walked back inside, then sent Mack her third related email about checking the Helmsman case records to see if a dead male was found inside. And then she started in on more research because there was so much to do.

As she sat here, she absentmindedly looked over at the folders still atop her kitchen table. Her gaze landed on the folder she had photocopied for Nan but hadn't been delivered yet. It was too late for Doreen to go to Rosemoor now. So she opened her copy of it and went through it, finding the transfer of title from many years ago on the property. Nan had bought the house from the Huntingtons. Brad and Jessica Huntington. Names that meant nothing to Doreen. But she wrote them down and started researching them. She had no idea where they went after selling their home or if they were even still alive.

She checked for the Huntington family in Kelowna online, and, sure enough, there was some mention of the name. As she continued to follow along, she found an obituary showing that the older couple had died, which was to be expected some forty-odd years later. The Huntingtons were survived by a son and daughter. She wondered at their ages, then reached for the local phone book and found a number for the son, Ron. She called before she gave herself a chance to stop. Ron answered. She explained who she was and said she was tracking down the family of someone named Veronica Phillips from the late 1890s or early 1900s.

"That's my great-grandmother, I think," Ron said. And when Doreen explained further about the hope chest, he sighed and said, "Well, it's possible, but I don't know for sure. As far as I understand, she remarried."

"Right," Doreen said. "What name do you know her as?"

"Veronica Huntington."

"Ah," she said. "I'll keep looking to see if I can find any research that says your Veronica Huntington is the Veronica I'm looking for."

"What was in this hope chest?" he asked curiously.

"Love letters. Lingerie from way back then, some dishes,

and maybe a tablecloth or two.”

“Ah, so nothing valuable then.”

“No clue, but it doesn’t look like anything was ever used. That’s why I was curious. It’s just an odd thing to find.”

“Sure, but in those old houses,” he said, “you could find anything.”

“True enough.” He appeared to be only interested if a big price tag was involved. In that case, Doreen was interested herself in these items. She rang off and jotted down notes. The thing was, his parents had owned this house. So did they have Veronica’s hope chest items from their grandmother or were they hanging on to it for somebody else? How was Doreen supposed to know? She should have asked Ron for his sister’s contact information. Doreen called him back and asked him about his sister.

“She passed away quite a while ago,” he said. “Breast cancer.”

“I’m sorry to hear that. So no one cares to see the love letters then, I presume?” she asked, feeling a heartbreaking disappointment.

“I doubt it,” Ron said. “That’s old stuff.”

“Yes,” she said. “It definitely is.”

When Doreen hung up, she felt a huge dissatisfaction with his answers. She understood his point because she hadn’t been at all interested in her own family’s antiques herself. But these love letters were so much more personal and so much more heartbreaking. She hadn’t asked if he had any aunts. She wanted to call him back once more, but figured his tolerance would not likely go too far. She researched his family tree instead. And she came across a Tina Huntington, Ron’s aunt, and the only other survivor of the family from that generation, if she was still alive.

Doreen found no address, phone number, or anything for anybody by that name. But, given her age, Doreen thought she might have another resource. She picked up the phone and called Nan.

As soon as she answered, Doreen said, "Tina Huntington?"

"What about her?" Nan asked, her voice slightly distracted.

"Do you know anything about her?"

"More than I'd like. She's a lousy gambler," Nan said crossly. "And she's always whining about her losses."

Doreen straightened. "You mean, she's at Rosemoor with you?"

"Yes, unfortunately," Nan snapped. "And she just lost a bet today. You should hear her complain. It's almost as if she's saying I cheated!"

"Oh, dear," Doreen said. "That sounds pretty rough."

"It is. That's the last thing I'd ever do. If people can't make up their minds about how to bet properly, then why is that my fault? Really, people just expect me to turn around and make them money."

"I'm sorry, Nan," Doreen said. "Is she of sound mind?"

Nan snorted at that. "Obviously not because, as I just said, she's accusing me of cheating."

Doreen rolled her eyes at that. "Well, she might be the only link to these hope chest boxes I found in the attic."

"Really?" Nan paused.

Doreen could hear Nan already shifting her track of thinking.

"Huntington," Nan said. "What does that have to do with anybody?"

Doreen explained, and Nan said, "Well, that would make Veronica her great-grandmother, right?"

"I think Veronica would be Tina's grandmother and then Tina's great-grandmother would be the woman who wrote the love letters, Veronica's mother."

"Oh, well. In that case, I'll have to talk to her about that," Nan said. "She won't want any of that stuff either. I can tell you that. Hates having any reminders of her family or her past around her. But I'll ask."

"I still don't know what I'm supposed to do with all that stuff then. It's not like anybody'll wear the clothing. It's too bad there isn't a historical society that I could donate it to. Is there? Something about early settlers?"

"It's possible," Nan said with sudden animation. "I might know somebody. I can ask about that too. Hold tight. Drat. I should ask Tina first though." *Click.*

Doreen stared at the phone, then laughed. "I thought I was the only one allowed to hang up on people."

Her grandmother called her back immediately though. "Tina wants nothing to do with it. So you're off the hook there. I'm still trying to get answers on the best place for you to donate those items, so leave it with me."

Well, that was an answer, maybe not the one she was looking for, but it helped to remove the last direct member of the family. Now it was all about finding the best home for the items.

Just then she heard a noise outside. She turned to look at Mugs, staring at the door. The hair on the back of his neck had risen, but he wasn't growling. In other words, he was confused and didn't understand what was going on. Well, that was okay; she was too. She walked to the front door, set the security alarm, and turned on the outside porch lights so she could take a look outside. Mugs was quiet at her side.

"We're back to needing a dictionary of animal signals," she muttered.

She went to the kitchen and opened the garage door, turning on the lights. It was empty, but, of course, the garage door on the other side wasn't locked. She still hadn't gotten that fixed. She went back to the kitchen, grabbed a chair, and jammed it under the doorknob. And then she did the same for her kitchen door. Sleeping tonight wasn't looking good.

As she went to bed, she considered sleeping on the living room floor. That wouldn't be very comfortable, and Mack would be seriously pissed at her for getting herself into so much trouble. But then a fire started on the ground floor did not give people on the second floor many options. She looked out the window and checked all around. With all the security set and the extra things she'd done, she was reasonably safe, but she knew it made no difference when it came to a fire.

As she thought about it more and more, she realized how much Penny would like Doreen to disappear. And Steve would too. But it had to look accidental. Yet any fire, especially arson, would point to all those other open arson cases. And Steve couldn't afford that. Neither could whatever remained of the biker gang he'd been dealing with.

When she woke in the middle of the night to the sounds of sirens, she bolted upright, her heart slamming against her chest. She held all the animals close to her, sure her house was on fire. Yet, as she sat here shivering in the cool evening air, she saw nothing but darkness around her.

No smoke curling. No flames.

Nothing but the darkness of night.

She shook the sleepiness from her brain and studied the neighborhood. There were fire engines, but they appeared to have gone down the road.

Her heart sank. Intuitively she knew what had happened. She got dressed, rearmed her security, and raced down toward Steve's house via the creek path. It was dark out, somewhere around four or five o'clock in the morning, but still not quite light enough to be sure of her footsteps. She tripped a couple times but caught herself before she fell. As soon as she came around the corner, she knew she was right because she could see the orange halo in the sky. She made it to the edge of the property and just stood here.

Steve's house was completely engulfed in flames.

And she knew his body would be inside.

# Chapter 26

*Wednesday Late Morning...*

DOREEN, ANIMALS IN tow, had come back several hours after watching the fire put out and crashed on the grass in her backyard, looking for a few hours of sleep in the early morning sunlight. She should have made it to her room, but she was afraid she was covered in smoke and knew she was too tired to take a shower right now. She dozed off and woke up to Mugs warming her on one side and Goliath on the other. Thaddeus had taken to sleeping on a weeping maple right beside her.

As she opened her eyes, she saw the tree was leafing out beautifully. It would be beautiful. She sat up, then groaned, her whole body aching and sore. Why was that? She looked down and saw the lumpy sod she'd been sleeping on. She stood and said, "We're heading in for a shower, guys."

She led her bedraggled family back inside and stepped into a hot shower. She stood under the water for a long moment, trying to shake off the terrible night so she could think. When she was dressed and back downstairs again, she made her coffee a little stronger than normal, thinking the caffeine might help. As she waited, her phone rang. It was

Mack. She groaned and said, "Good morning, Mack."

"You sound terrible."

"Thanks. I appreciate that," she said sarcastically.

His voice changed. "Are you okay?"

"Outside of the fact that Steve's house burned to the ground last night, I'm fine," she snapped.

"I wondered if you'd heard."

"I bolted out of my house in the middle of the night when I heard the sirens. So I have you to blame for my lousy night's sleep." Then she smiled. Of course, he wasn't to blame—it was Steve's house on fire that had necessitated the sirens. But it was a great way to bug Mack.

There was a shocked snort on the other side. "You're welcome," he said. "Remember that part about not getting yourself into danger?"

"Yeah," she said. "Remember that part about not scaring me unnecessarily?"

"It's hardly unnecessarily when Steve's house just burned to the ground," he said quietly.

She winced. "All right, you get a point for that one. I'm not very awake. I fell asleep on the grass after I got home from watching the firemen work, and I'm still waiting for this very slow coffeepot to make me coffee to kick me awake."

He chuckled, his voice low, deep, and husky. "I wish I could have seen that."

She cracked a smile. "You probably would have been hollering at me, but Mugs was curled up on one side while Goliath was on the other. Thaddeus was on the closest tree. So it was definitely a fun way to wake up. I'm exhausted though."

"I'm sure you are," he said. "But maybe we can get some

answers now."

"I figured that Steve was probably dead inside his house. Have you heard reports of that yet?"

"Not yet," he said. "I'm there now."

"What?" She straightened and looked at the coffeepot. "Why didn't you tell me?"

"I'm a cop, remember? I'm checking out the circumstances of the fire."

"I can tell you the fire started well after midnight because the sirens woke me about four or five a.m. And, for sure, you'll find a male body in the house."

*Silence.* "Do you really think so?"

"Hell yes. Like you said, a cheetah never changes his spots."

"I didn't say that," he said. "And the phrase is, a *leopard never changes his spots.*"

She waved her hand in the air. "Whatever. You said this would happen."

"No, I said it would likely happen to you, and I thought Steve would skip town."

"I don't think he acted fast enough," she said. Finally, the coffeemaker beeped in front of her, and she grabbed the pot and poured herself a cup. Then she stepped outside into the early morning sun. "He probably told somebody about my file and got himself killed for his carelessness."

"You could be right about that," he said, his voice thoughtful. "Which means you're next."

She glared at her phone. "I've already had a night from hell, so, if you're using your scare tactics again, I really don't need it."

"I'm not using scare tactics," Mack snapped. "Be sensible. If a body is found in this fire scene, and, if it's Steve, it only makes sense that you could be the next victim."

"There have been no other victims in the last twenty-plus years, so I highly doubt it'll be an issue." The thing was, she knew Mack was right. She just didn't want to admit it; there'd be no living with him if she did.

"You do have fire insurance on the house, right?" Mack asked.

"Yes," she said. "I asked Nan yesterday." And then she realized what she had said.

He chuckled. "At least you're taking it seriously. Or at least a little bit seriously."

"I'm taking it seriously, but there's a limit to how seriously I can."

"Just take it easy. Have a couple cups of coffee, and maybe I'll stop by when I'm done here."

"Good. I need an update." Just then she yawned loud and long. And she groaned and said, "I'm getting off now." And she hung up. Even hanging up on him again made her smile. She walked out to the front porch steps and sipped the strong black coffee.

As soon as it hit her throat and moved down to her stomach, she let out a happy sigh. "This might be the devil's brew, but I'm definitely in heaven right now."

# Chapter 27

*Wednesday Noonish ...*

DOREEN HAD GONE through more of Nan's unorganized paperwork, sorted it out, put aside another stack she had to take to Nan to confirm whether to toss this stuff or to save it. Otherwise, as far as she could see, everything else was done in the house. And, even if the place did burn down now—God forbid—all the files from Solomon had been put into digital format, so they would at least always be there. She refilled her coffee and went out to the deck to enjoy it.

She hadn't had a chance to look into her other mystery that also interested her, the newspaper clippings from Nan's friend on Bob Little. Or was it Bob Small? Brian Small? She shook her head, her brain too confused to even remember that much. She had more than enough to work on without adding anything else.

The prime problem now was Steve. She wanted names for all those people who'd been paid off. The trouble was, if the payout was also so they would disappear, then the biker gang had done a good job of it. Because no one seemed to know where these widows had gone; they hadn't been heard from again. Doreen wondered, *Or did they?* Maybe they hadn't. Maybe they'd been *helped* to disappear. Had those checks ever been cashed? She sat here on the deck, pondering that, when she heard a voice out front.

When Mack walked into the front door of the house, Doreen felt somewhat better. But not necessarily a whole lot. She called out, "I'm in the back."

Mack walked outside to join her, and she looked at him. "That didn't take long."

"I'd been there since about six o'clock this morning," he said. "So now we're waiting for reports from the fire chief and the coroner."

"*Coroner*," she said, jumping on it.

His face was grim as he nodded and said, "There was a body. A single male in the house."

"Aha!" She stabbed the air with a finger in his direction. "See? I told you so."

He glared at her. "Yeah, I know. It's not nice to say, *I told you so*."

"But I tell you, you need to investigate one other thing a little closer …"

"And what is it you think needs to be investigated?"

"If those checks he supposedly handed over to those women were ever cashed."

Mack stopped, twisted in place, and looked at her. His eyebrows shot up.

She nodded. "Wouldn't it be nice to know that?"

"You're thinking that, if they weren't cashed, the women weren't around to take them to the bank?"

"Steve doesn't strike me as somebody who'd waste money on a deal like that. What if later one of the women decides to talk? Or if all the women get together and decide to talk?

Steve would have to worry about that forever. But … not if he can dispose of the women and at the same time keep the money for himself."

"You have a very devious and twisted mind."

She beamed at him. "Thank you."

"I'm not sure that's something you should be thanking me for."

"You can check though, can't you?"

"Potentially. But you're right. It's a good line of inquiry." He motioned at her coffee cup and asked, "Is that the end of the pot?"

"Yes," she said, scrambling to her feet to get inside before he could. She poured herself the final coffee in the pot. He turned and looked at her in outrage. She smirked. "You can put on the next pot."

He snorted at that and said, "Are you that desperate?"

"I'm not kidding," she said. "I woke up on the grass outside."

He made another pot of coffee and turned to look at her. "Can you sleep here tonight?"

"I'm not sure," she said. "There's something really wrong in this town."

"We didn't think anything was wrong with this town," he said, a note of humor in his voice, "until you showed up. And then, of course, that changed everything."

"Yeah. Apparently, I'm a nosy body who can't stop getting into people's faces. Oh, and what happened to Crystal?"

"She's on her way home, but a snag in the paperwork caused a few delays. We're hoping she'll be here by the coming weekend."

"Good," Doreen said. "I'm sure the town will be delighted."

"If you think Steve," Mack said, looking at her as he leaned against the counter and waited for the pot to drip, "had something to do with those women not cashing their checks, what do you think he did with the money?"

"It depends how desperate he was for cash," she said. "Because to hire somebody to kill these men and their wives and to then hire an arsonist meant Steve had to pay these people. It also meant now these people would know about it. But what if he invited these people to his house and killed them there? Have you seen the size of his property? It's huge."

Mack stared at her, then looked out at the vast expanse of her backyard and her own gardening that she didn't want to be reminded of. Then he nodded. "It's possible, but he'd be taking a hell of a chance."

"Not really. Just think about it. Everybody thinks the best of him. You know yourself what a proper image can do to make you squeaky clean in the eyes of the law and to the public. Nobody would even have thought of it."

"But he must have waited to kill their wives, in order to allay suspicion, except he'd have to do it soon enough they didn't cash their checks. And burying them is no guarantee the police dogs wouldn't find them."

"Well, if he'd done it right," she said, "it wouldn't have been very difficult either."

"No, … not at all," he said. "Because Steve did a big addition on that property many years back, but I can't remember when."

She looked at him and said, "And that would likely mean heavy equipment."

He nodded. "It would, but we don't have any reason to suspect these women are missing. There have been no missing-persons reports filed on them.”

“That you know of,” she said. “Have you checked?”

“Yes,” he said. “Remember how I’m a cop? I read the files, and the cops assigned to those cases initially checked for the wives’ names. I did a follow-up check for those names, and they do not come up in the database.”

“But it’s been twenty-two years ago, right? How good are the search parameters? What were their maiden names and did their families even know they were married?” And then she stopped and asked, “And where were they married?”

“What difference does that make?”

“Think about how common-law marriage is handled in Canada. I’ve heard tales about how they are ruled by different standards, depending where you live in Canada. You must know more about it though. However, if the men died, and they owned the houses back then, and, if they weren’t married, then the women wouldn’t get anything out of the house or any life insurance. If that even existed.”

He sat down beside her. “True,” he said. “So that would explain why Steve was helping them with a check.”

“Exactly,” Doreen said.

“I’ll have to think on this and go back to the database,” Mack said. Then he pinched his nose and rubbed at the bridge. “Some sleep would help too.”

Doreen felt sorry for him. “You’re right,” she said. “I had a choice about going back to my bed, but you didn’t. Sorry.”

“No,” he said. “And apparently, I was forced to come here and listen to more of your theories over coffee.” But at least the note of humor had come back into his voice. “Except without the coffee.”

“Coffee is done. Help yourself.” She smiled and said,

"Besides, with these cases, you need a fresh eye."

"No," he said. "It's not even a fresh eye. It's about having something new to break the case open. And, in this case, that's just what happened. Because it's Steve's property, and it was arson, and there's a male body, now we can tear his life apart. We had no reason to suspect him and no evidence to point to him as the guilty party."

"But now," she said with a smirk, "you can take him down."

"There's no point in taking him down," he reminded her. "The man's already down. He'll only be going six feet farther."

Doreen winced at that. "True, but a lot of families could be involved in a lot of related cold cases."

Mack groaned at that, then laughed. "The guys already want me to stop you from digging into these cold cases. You've caused everybody a lot of work."

"They're not serious, are they?" She hoped they were joking. The last thing she wanted to believe was the extra work overrode doing the right thing.

He shook his head. "No, they're not. They're loving this as much as anybody."

"Good," Doreen said, "because I'd really hate to think that any cop didn't want these cases closed."

"No, not happening."

# Chapter 28

*Wednesday Midafternoon …*

BY MIDAFTERNOON, DOREEN went back to bed and took a nap. When she woke up for the third time today, she felt refreshed, like she might make it through the rest of the day. She got up and made herself one of the biggest sandwiches she'd ever had. Feeding a little bit of the ham and cheese to Goliath and Mugs and a little bit of her lettuce to Thaddeus, her group ate in peaceful contentedness.

Except her mind buzzed with the ideas. If Steve was dead, that would be a huge blow to Penny. Doreen was pretty sure that, in Penny's mind, Steve would be her savior and would get her out of this. Now that her husband, George, wasn't here to help her out of her tough spots, she'd been likely relying on Steve for support. If dead, that wouldn't happen now.

With her mind rolling through ideas, Doreen pulled a pad of paper and a pen toward her and jotted them down. If the checks came back as cashed, then that theory, of course, went out the window. But why were there no files on these women? Or were they all women in a vulnerable position? And then Doreen thought about it and realized the women in these gangs were often separated from their families and lived a precarious lifestyle anyway. Their birth families probably had no idea where they were or how they were living at the time this all went down—short of the women themselves contacting their families for help.

Yet, if these women had been with these men for any time period, would they call their families? Doreen highly doubted it. But maybe that was a possibility. And that brought her around to that original case of arson. The man in the Kelowna gang who had been killed first and likely led to the other three fires and deaths in retaliation. As far she was concerned, that first fire had started this ugly cycle. That was the Helmsman case. Where was his wife?

Doreen did as much research as she could, finding an Annette Helmsman who had survived that fire. Further research didn't give much information though. But when Doreen researched the family name, she did get a hit. There were a couple possible spellings listed in Kelowna. But Helmsman wouldn't have been *her* name if they weren't married.

If they *were* married, then maybe she didn't need a big check from Steve because she would have gotten a life insurance payout or even a house insurance reimbursement. Still, a life insurance policy on a biker was a big leap. They probably couldn't afford that. Plus, Doreen couldn't confirm the check angle either. And Mack was no help on that as well.

Thinking about that, she dialed the number of the name with the first spelling. The person who answered sounded confused, told her, "Sorry, you must have the wrong number." Doreen thanked the person and looked up the second spelling. There she got an irritated man, saying,

"She's not at this number anymore."

"Do you happen to know where she is?"

"She's in a hospice," he said. "But I don't know where."

At that, Doreen put down her phone and thought of hospices. So, somewhere like where Solomon was. But not likely the same place. That would be too much of a coincidence. There was a hospice society in town though. She picked up the phone and called, then asked about Annette Helmsman's condition and if visitors were allowed. The woman on the other end said, "Only if Annette wants to see the visitor. Generally, it's restricted to friends and family."

"Oh," Doreen said. "Right. I don't even know where she is."

"The Giusichan Hospice Center."

"Okay, interesting. Thank you. I'll phone and see if Annette would like a visitor."

"Some of these people are very lonely, so I'm sure she'd be grateful."

Thanking the woman, Doreen rang off and then looked up the number for the hospice. Then she made yet another call.

"Annette doesn't get many visitors," said the woman who answered. "I can talk to her. Or do you want me to patch her through?"

"Sure," Doreen said. At that, the phone rang, and another person picked up the phone.

"Hello?"

This was a very old and weak voice. Doreen was surprised she had access to the phone herself. But, if it were Nan, no way in heck would she allow anybody to take away her independence by keeping a phone from her.

Doreen introduced herself and said, "I'm looking into

the death of your partner from way back then."

"Oh my," Annette said, then was quiet before continuing in a frail voice. "You know what? Somebody needs to hear the truth. Are you that bone lady?"

Doreen smiled and said, "Yes, I am."

"Can you get the animals in here?"

Doreen winced. "Is there an outside patio where I could meet you? I don't think they'll let animals into the medical facility."

Annette's voice faded slightly, and she said, "There is a veranda. But I don't want to be alone there."

"Why don't I come down first, and then I'll see if I can get permission to bring the animals to meet you?"

"Sure," Annette said, her voice gaining in strength. "Bring a recorder. I don't have too much time left on this earth. My younger years weren't the best."

Although her voice was gaining in strength, and she no longer sounded like she was at death's door, it still had a heavy breathlessness to it. "When do you want me to come?"

"Tomorrow morning. That is, if I make it through the night."

At that, Doreen rang off, now worried about Annette. What were the chances she wouldn't make it until the morning?

It was late afternoon only, and Doreen knew it would test her patience to wait until tomorrow morning, but what she also needed was to be prepared. She decided that, instead of using her cell phone as a recorder, she should probably get something a bit better. She hopped into her vehicle and went into town. An electronics store was by the mall, and yet, another little shop was off Glenmore. She went for the mall.

She was shown something for less than thirty dollars.

But it was still money. She hemmed and hawed and then decided it could be important. She bought it and found out she needed batteries for it, so she bought a pack of those.

Back home again, she tested it out several times. And then, with that and her phone and her notepad ready and waiting, she still had the rest of the evening to get through. And the best thing for that was hard work. But groaning, she wasn't sure she had enough energy for gardening. Still, while she had daylight, she took the animals and this time a fresh cup of tea and went outside and started digging up weeds. If she could at least dig back another couple feet, she'd feel like she'd done something. She worked hard for a couple hours and then collapsed on the grass.

"That's it," she said to Mugs, flopping onto her back. "I'm done."

He woofed and sat in her lap, rolling up so his big thick paws were in the sky. She scratched his belly and just spent a few moments cuddling him. Her tea had long gone cold. Her sandwich had been long-ago digested too, and she was fading quickly. She needed some way to destress and to relax before falling asleep.

She remembered the four books she still had. Grabbing one, she set it on the kitchen table. It was too early to go to bed, but maybe with a light dinner in her room, she could relax and read. So, that was what she did. By nine o'clock, she crashed into her bed.

# Chapter 29

*Thursday Morning ...*

WHEN DOREEN WOKE up the next morning, she was relieved she'd slept so well and so long, even with lingering fears of her house burning to the ground in the middle of the night.

She made coffee, checked her time, and would leave soon to see Annette. Doreen had to drive, which meant locking up the animals again. Annette had wanted to see them, but Doreen wasn't prepared to take them to the hospice without prior permission from the management. She could easily bring them on a second visit.

She set the alarm and escaped, hating the long sad looks from the animals. Particularly Mugs, who often got to come with her more than the other two. At least the media appeared to have completely disappeared now. If she could only stay out of trouble, they might not return. Finally clear of the cul-de-sac, she drove the few miles to the hospice.

Along the way, Doreen wondered how to open this conversation and how to get the answers she needed without upsetting a very sick woman, but there was no way to know beforehand. She'd just have to dive in.

She walked into the front entrance and checked what room Annette was in. With the correct room number, Doreen followed instructions and knocked. When the voice called out, "Come in," Doreen stepped inside to see a woman who looked like she'd had her heart and soul taken away from her, and she was totally done for. Doreen smiled and said, "I'm Doreen, the bone lady."

Annette smiled. "I'm Annette. Although you're not a priest, I do feel like I need to have a moment to confess to somebody. All I ask is that you don't share this information until after I'm gone."

Knowing that would be damn hard to do since the information could save a life, Doreen said, "I agree." She could only hope—and she hated thinking about that—that Annette wouldn't stay long in this world.

Annette seemed to read her mind. "Not to worry. I won't be around in a few days anyway."

Doreen sat down and turned on the recorder. "I'm sorry to hear that. But I understand how facing that can make us have regrets."

Annette nodded.

"Okay. What is it you'd like to tell the world?"

"I, Annette Helmsman," the woman started, her eyes closed, "of sound mind and a failing body, am giving a dissertation on my life and all the problems of my past. I was part of the Devil Riders' gang out of Kelowna when I married my husband. Although he was part of the gang too, I hadn't realized just what that life would bring. But I was a willing cohort and agreed to the lifestyle, despite it being rough and not all of it to my liking. We'd only been married eight years when he was killed in a house fire. My life changed afterward.

"I was still part of the gang and was looked after to a certain extent, but I no longer belonged to anyone in particular and was passed around until I could find another partner. I didn't know how to leave the gang, and I didn't know how to exist in that new world without my partner, so I just survived until something changed so that I could get out of the gang.

"But getting out of the gang didn't happen until almost twenty years later, and since then, over these last two years, my life has been a lot easier. But that's also when my body decided to turn on me from the years of abuse. I have pancreatic cancer and do not expect to live out this week." She fell silent for a long moment.

Doreen didn't know if she should prompt Annette or just let her words flow.

Finally, Annette picked up the pace. "My husband's gang brothers wanted retaliation for his death. They were adamant that his death was caused by another gang that had moved into the area. They murdered men and then burned houses to the ground of four separate families. Yes, before you ask, all of them were members of the other gang. I don't know the names of the men or of their wives."

Her voice became faint. "Years later I understood how life was different if you weren't part of the gang like that. For my part in those killings, I know there is no asking for forgiveness."

"What was your part in those killings?" Doreen asked, trying to keep the conversation flowing yet shocked at what she heard.

"I drove one of the getaway vehicles," she said. "I knew what they were doing as they headed in. I knew the women would be spared, but that's about all."

"You were in a *biker* gang," Doreen said, hesitating, "so why did you drive a car?"

"So that nobody knew it was a gang hit," she said.

"Who was responsible for killing these four men?"

"Our gang leader." Annette gasped for breath. "T-Bone. And his two lieutenants, Red and Manny."

"Did you see them kill these men?"

She shook her head—or tried to. "No. But I drove those three men each time to the houses of their four victims."

"All these fires were relatively close together," Doreen said. "Why?"

"There was one a week for four weeks. Every Monday. Because T-Bone wanted their victims to start the week off hating what was to come."

Doreen didn't understand that thinking, but there wasn't a lot she could say about it. "How were the men killed?"

"They were … No," she stopped, looked confused for a moment, and then said, "They were stabbed in the gut. Soft tissue not to nick the bone. Then their bodies and their houses were lit."

"And the women—where were they?"

"They were all told to get out of town or to face the same consequences. For that matter, so were the men. But they didn't believe it. And they didn't listen. But then to walk out of town would have made them look like cowards. So, of course, they couldn't."

"And the women were all paid afterward. Why?"

"Because the Devil Riders' gang knew they would make trouble otherwise."

"But how does that work? You said the women were with the gang and that made them part of it, whether with the Devil Riders or the rival gang, right? So why did your gang care about their livelihood afterward?"

"That was Steve's idea. The Devil Riders fought it for a long time. And then decided, what the hell? Particularly when they found out one of the women was pregnant. They figured the woman, once giving birth, would want more money or would want retaliation of her own." Annette gave a half a snort that ended up closer to a cough. "Steve gave me money too, but it wasn't enough to rebuild a new life outside of the gang."

Doreen winced. "I'm sorry to hear that. Do you know where any of the women went?"

"No," Annette said, her voice strained. "The agreement was that they were to leave town and to never be seen again."

All Doreen could think of was how convenient that was. "And is there anything else you need to make peace with?" she asked Annette.

"Only that I'm sorry for everything I had to do with it," she said. "Life wasn't easy back then. I did anything I could to survive. And it was a far cry from the life I finally had when I was away from the gang. But now all my sins have caught up with me, and my body is making me pay."

"I'm sorry," Doreen said. "It can't be easy for you."

The woman shook her head. "No, it's not," she whispered. "But I have come to understand some of it." Then her voice fell silent.

Doreen waited for her to say something else, but the woman's eyes slowly closed, and her breathing deepened. Doreen shut off the recorder and stood, then snuck out of the room. As she left, she whispered, "I'll call you later."

She walked out to the front hall; she smiled at the receptionist and said, "Thank you. Annette is sleeping again."

"Good," the woman said. "She didn't want her painkillers this morning so she could talk to you."

"How long does she really have?"

"Five days maximum," the receptionist said. "But her will is strong. Honestly, we all thought she'd be dead a few weeks ago, but something was bothering her. Hopefully whatever she wanted to discuss with you has helped."

"I hope so," Doreen said with a gentle smile. "I can't think of anything worse than going to the grave carrying secrets that terrify you. Is there any chance I could bring my pets down here if I come back? Annette did ask me to bring them this time…"

The receptionist shook her head. "Sorry, it's against our policy. They'd have to be registered therapy animals."

She thanked the woman and walked out into the morning sun, feeling almost a dirtiness from the confession. She got in her vehicle and drove home. Something about seeing life from another perspective and realizing how unhappy the woman had been and how ravaged she was by her disease made Doreen grateful for the life she had with Nan and her animals.

She pulled into her driveway, used her automatic door opener to open the garage, and drove her car in. She smiled as she got out, then closed the big double door, and walked to the kitchen door but realized she had locked the door with a chair. Groaning, she had to let herself out of the big door, closing it again using the keypad, and then walked around to the front door.

Peering inside the big picture window to the living room, she could see Mugs going nuts because somebody had gone into the garage. Although he probably recognized the sound of her car, he didn't understand what was happening.

The door opener was also a new thing to him. It was a new thing to her as well. The remote had been in the garage the whole time, but it hadn't worked until Mack had fiddled with it. And she hadn't even realized he'd done that until he handed her the remote and told her how to use it.

She walked to the front door, unlocked it to shut it again, disarmed the security system, and sat down on the floor. The critters rushed to her, and she cuddled them.

"When I die," she announced, "let it be fast. And let it not make you guys' life tough."

When she finally gave everybody the loving they needed, she rose and headed into the kitchen to make herself a cup of tea. Something was so sad about Annette. There'd been no mention of a child, no mention of a family, no mention of anyone who cared. And even the receptionist said she didn't get many visitors. And that was even sadder.

But now Doreen had something major she needed to deal with. While the kettle boiled, she opened her laptop and plugged in the recorder, hoping against hope it had worked. Then she copied it to her laptop and stored it in the cloud.

After that, she listened to Annette's raspy voice. Her pain filled the kitchen. With that, Doreen copied it and sent it to her new email for safekeeping. How could she possibly not tell Mack? It wouldn't hurt anybody at this stage of the game, and it was definitely important as far as these arson cases were concerned.

Just then Mack, maybe even knowing she was thinking about him, called her. She sighed happily. "Hey," she said.

"Hey," he said. "You sound different."

"Yes. I just listened to a dying woman's confession," she said sadly. "It's painful, and I promised her I wouldn't let anybody else know until she passes."

"Confession of what?" he asked, his voice harsh.

She winced, took a deep breath, and let the words come out in a rush. "Her part in four murders."

# Chapter 30

*Thursday Late Morning ...*

DOREEN WAITED THROUGH Mack's silence, holding her breath. Her face was already scrunched up, and he didn't disappoint.

"What?" he roared. "Are you serious?"

"Yes," she said in a small voice. "I'm sorry."

"Sorry?" he asked, still irate. "Sorry for what?"

"Because I can't tell you anything yet."

There was more stunned silence, and Mack said, "Please tell me this doesn't have anything to do with the current cases?"

She winced and whispered, "I cannot tell a lie."

He groaned a loud and drawn-out angry groan. "You will be the death of me," he snapped. Then he hung up.

"Well, that went well," she said to the animals gathered around her. They all had worried looks on their faces. And how was it she even knew that? Except that, by now, she understood some of their expressions. Mugs's face hung even lower, while Goliath stared at her like she'd done something terrible. Even Thaddeus gave her the gimlet-eyed look.

She groaned. "Well, what am I supposed to do? Somehow I'm supposed to keep a promise, and it never even occurred to me what a promise I was keeping until I heard the confession. But I can understand Annette's point of view too."

She got up, grabbed a cup of tea, and sat on the deck. As much as she hated to say it, it would be a good thing if Helmsman passed away in the night. And how awful to wish for. It was terrible. But, unable to help herself, she called the hospice center and asked about Annette.

"She's not doing well," the woman said. "She's not taking visitors, and we're not patching through phone calls."

"Okay," Doreen said softly. "I gather the end is not far away."

"There's no way to know for sure," the woman said. "We all work on the assumption that every day is a new day." On that, she hung up and left Doreen staring at the phone.

"I know it's not nice to think about," she said, "but, Annette, if you're suffering and in pain and are ready to go, I do hope you get to go earlier than later." But she felt terrible because Annette's death really did have a lot to do with Mack and did have to do with these cases. And somehow Doreen was supposed to work her way through this moral conflict because she had promised. But did a promise matter when you didn't understand the full extent of your promise before you heard all the details?

Before, rights and wrongs had always been easy for her. She'd understand what to do and when to do it. But now, she knew that morally it was wrong to tell Mack, but ethically it was the right thing to do. And that just made her conflicted. When she heard a car door slam out front, Thaddeus whispered in a very low voice, "Mack is here.

Mack is here."

She gave him a startled look, bounced to her feet, and raced to the end of the backyard to stand at the creek. She could hope it wasn't Mack, but, in her heart of hearts, she knew it was, and it would be the towering and angry Mack.

She couldn't really blame him. She was withholding vital information on a current case—Steve's case—and four old cases. And that was just too unbelievable that Annette wanted to confess. To Doreen. Was it timing? Was it Doreen's demeanor? Or was it now Doreen's reputation as the bone lady that had let this woman decide to confess all? Or was it the fact that Annette was facing death in an uncertain future and wanted to clear her conscious? Any and all of those answers weren't good enough for Mack.

Behind her, she heard a roar. "Doreen?"

She hunched her shoulders. She knew there was no way to get out of this. She would have to face the music. "I just hope he understands," she murmured.

"Not happening. Not happening." Thaddeus went off in a cackling chuckle. He'd gone from rock to rock, as if caught up in an uncertain energy.

She glared at him. "Well, it could."

She turned and watched Mack stride toward her from her back deck, the kitchen door banging hard behind him. His fists were clenched, his shoulders stiff, his expression irate, and his skin almost cherry red. As soon as he approached, she frowned at him. "You need some stress relief. You'll have a heart attack."

He opened his mouth, but what came out was nothing. He snapped his mouth closed, inhaled, then said, "*You* will be the death of me."

She nodded. "And I'm so sorry. I've been thinking my

way through this thing, but I had no clue what was being dumped on my plate. I've decided it's morally wrong to tell you, but it's ethically right to tell you."

He stared at her. "Seriously?"

She nodded. "Well, I'm hoping, if I give you a little hint, you can guess."

He showed her what he had in his hand. Her recorder. "Does it have something to do with this?"

She looked at him in surprise and nodded. "Yes, it does. How did you know?"

"Because I know how you operate, and this was a new item I saw on the table as I came through," he said.

While she stared at him in stunned surprise, he hit Play.

"No!"

But it was too late. Helmsman's voice rolled through. Doreen's shoulders sagged, and she shrugged. "You see? That's the thing about devils like you. It takes away my decision-making."

"Shouldn't have been a decision at all," he said.

She gave him a haunted look. "She made me promise."

His face softened ever-so-slightly until he heard the confession.

She nodded. "That's why I was thinking that ethically I needed to tell you."

"You think?" he asked sarcastically. Then he held up a hand as he listened to Annette's version of the fires and her part in it. He shook his head. "Good Lord." He let it continue to play, but he rubbed his face with his free hand, as if tired beyond belief.

And she could well imagine he was. Since she'd arrived, there had been no peace. She couldn't believe how much chaos had overtaken her world.

She was still trying to figure out if this was how everybody lived and how her life before had been so simple and empty because her husband had never let her do anything. Would she have gotten into the same amount of trouble if he had lessened his control over her? She couldn't imagine it. He would have frowned on her being involved in anything so nasty as a murder.

It wasn't ladylike, even though she had certainly seen enough of his business dealings to know they were criminal in nature or at least slimy. And he had peculiar ideas about women and enough power to enforce them. What made the difference between one criminal act and another?

Finally, the voice drifted off, and nothing more was heard on the recorder.

In a low voice, Doreen said, "That's when she drifted off to sleep again. And I checked in just recently, and she's not doing well."

He nodded. "As in, she can't be a questioned?"

"I don't think so," she said. "As in, I think she probably won't be of this world today or tomorrow."

Mack stared out at the creek. "This changes things."

"It changes a lot of things," Doreen said, "but, in many ways, it changes nothing."

"And that's the problem with cold cases. I have to look in the files and run names to see if anybody's still alive." He raised the recorder in his hand and said, "This is the clearest and most concise account of anything we have from back then."

"Even Steve's dead," she said, "but I don't know who set his house fire."

"It's possible that he did," Mack said.

"Oh," she said with a frown. "I never considered that."

"If he thought the end was coming, and he didn't want to face the music and have his reputation ruined, not to mention those who were closest to him would know exactly what he had been involved in, he could have done it. You know what? You have to consider it as that's an easy way out."

"Maybe," she said softly. "But not so easy."

"Maybe not, but, if he poured the accelerant all around his property and set it afire, it's pretty hard to have second thoughts."

"Yes," she whispered. Her mind was filled with images of Steve and his house burning around him and knowing he was on his own. She groaned. "It's not what I would have thought of him, but who knows? He always operated in the shadows, so it's hard to say just how bad and how far gone he was mentally."

"Are you thinking he had dementia or something?" Mack asked.

She shook her head. "No, I meant morally."

"You seem to be having moral and ethical issues today."

"I did get a little slap in my face about it," Doreen said. "I was concerned when Helmsman fell asleep like she did. That's why I was checking up on her just a few minutes ago. Now, honestly, I'm not sure if she'll even wake up. It's almost as if she took one heavy sigh with the burden off her chest and found peace."

"It does happen that way," Mack said. He walked a few steps away, pulled out his phone, and made a call. His gaze was gentle as he turned to her afterward. "As a matter of fact, that's exactly what she has done. She passed about twenty minutes ago."

"But I just called."

"The receptionist probably hadn't gotten word yet. And you're not the police."

Doreen glared at him but appreciated the differences.

"Well, it's a good thing I went this morning, isn't it?" She pointed at the recorder. "And just in case you're wondering, there's an email on my laptop with that attached to go to you sitting in my Drafts folder."

"Damn good thing," he said. "And how did you happen to connect with her?"

Doreen shrugged and gave him the story.

He groaned. "Of course, and the fact that she knew you were the bone lady meant you were the perfect person to talk to."

"I would think most people with her lifestyle back then are hesitant to talk to the police. Even now."

"You're right. Some aversions just never go away, even when you're dying. But it's sad because she could have relieved herself of this burden a long time ago."

"Maybe, but I think people have to do what they have to do when it feels right."

Mack stood there and asked, "Is that a personal observation on your own life?"

She thought about it. "You know what? It's hard to even think about that. But maybe?"

He nodded. Then he asked, "What about a chance of coffee?"

"Sure," she said. "Does that mean we're friends again?"

He snorted. "Until the next time."

She laughed. And then she told him about what Thaddeus had done. He looked at her in astonishment, then looked over at Thaddeus, who waddled behind them, happy and carefree.

"He knew it was me?" he asked.

"He might have recognized that particular slam to your car door," she said with an airy movement of her hand. "It's not like we haven't heard it a time or two."

He laughed. "Wouldn't it be nice if I didn't have to do it again?"

"Wouldn't it?" she agreed. "But chances are, you will."

# Chapter 31

*Thursday Noon ...*

IN THE KITCHEN, Mack put on the coffee, while Doreen sat down and sent off the email to him that she had already drafted. "Okay," she said. "You have a digital copy."

"Good," he said as he opened her fridge.

She watched him in surprise. "Are you hungry?"

He snorted. "Always. But we'd planned spaghetti for Friday. Unless you want it tonight, and we can have leftovers tomorrow?"

She stared at him. "Spaghetti twice is always a good idea."

"So let's check to see if you have the ingredients we need." He checked it all out, nodded, and said, "Perfect."

"Good," she said. "But we don't need to start yet, right?"

"No. Not until later this afternoon. I'm still recovering from almost no sleep last night. That's why the coffee. After this, I'll go back and start dealing with this case. Obviously, we need to take a new look at all the evidence."

"Yes, but honestly, that's four more cold cases," she said in a singsong voice, "plus Steve's current case."

He slowly turned and glared at her.

She wiped the smile off her face and batted her eyelashes at him instead.

He chuckled. "As much as we appreciate it …"

"I know," she said. "I'm making you guys look like idiots."

At his glare, she laughed, holding her hands in front of her in a gesture of conciliation. "I'm joking."

He nodded. "Better. The fact is, you have a knack for this, and, for whatever reason, people are coming to you too."

"That's not a bad thing," she said. "I'm sorry you guys get stuck with all the paperwork."

"It's okay," he said. "We're happy to see the closure for all these cases too."

"Right," she said. "And I still have a couple other things to work on."

"Like?"

"Like finding maybe a memorial society or a pioneering society or whatever for all those hope chest items."

"All of them?"

"I'm not sure. I was thinking definitely the nightgowns and the love letters. Maybe some of the dishes, but I don't know."

"I would contact Scott first about that set of dishes," Mack said. "If it's not worth anything, then donate it all."

"Or," she said with a wry look on her face, "maybe I'll keep it as a good set for myself."

He looked at her in surprise and nodded. "I like that idea. Why not have yourself a Sunday set of dishes? At least somebody'll use them after however many decades they've been sitting here."

"You mean, more than one century?"

He rolled his eyes. "If that's the case, that would be very sad. And I highly doubt the original owner of all those items would mind if you found joy in stuff she had collected for her own wedding."

"I like the idea," Doreen said softly. Then her practical side returned, and she said, "Unless Scott says something to convince me otherwise."

He chuckled. "Always the pragmatist."

"I was broke just long enough," she said, "that I saw that cliff of poverty and realized how closely poised I was to fall over the edge. If it wasn't for Nan, I would have hit that bottom real fast."

"But you didn't because of your nan," he said gently. "And honestly, a lot of people end up doing very well because of their family. If it isn't an inheritance, it's a helping hand."

"I know. Once again I find myself almost tearful over what Nan did for me."

"Then maybe this afternoon you should take a walk down there. Give her something for a change instead of letting her send you home with something."

She looked at him and then realized what he was saying. "Oh my," she said, jumping to her feet, her hand to her chest. "Do you think I've been taking advantage of her?" She looked around at her kitchen. "Oh, now I feel terrible."

"Whoa, whoa, whoa," Mack said. He reached out to gently grab her by her shoulders. "That's not what I meant. But you have received so much, and, although I highly doubt Nan's looking for anything, she might appreciate a little something too."

Doreen sat down on her butt and nodded. "I haven't done enough for her. I need to spend more time with her."

"Or you might want to remember she has a life," he said in a wry tone. "So don't expect her to want to spend more time with you, but that doesn't mean you can't deliver flowers."

She smiled at him. "You're better at this than I am."

"Better at what?"

"Relationships," she said. "I had very little to do with anybody. I hardly know the nuances. Oh, I understood the politeness of taking a good bottle of burgundy or red wine whenever we went to a dinner party, and I knew exactly how to thank everybody for a disgusting dinner on some occasions. I also understood how to save face and how to make everything appear to be perfect on the surface. But *real* relationships, like what I have with Nan—and dare I say, the friendship we have—I don't have much experience with."

Mack leaned against the kitchen counter and crossed his arms over his chest. "That's a really interesting insight. I would definitely say what we have is real. I feel like I can honestly yell at you and tell you off when I need to. But, then again, you apparently feel totally okay hanging up on me on a regular basis."

She snickered. "Well, it's not quite passive-aggressiveness—which was all I was ever allowed to be—and never even that much because my ex shot me down for it. But I do feel free to tell you how I feel from time to time."

He rolled his eyes. "Good, because I would hate to think you were pandering to me."

She shook her head. "Not happening. The animals might though if it got them a treat."

He looked at them to see Thaddeus staring at him. "What do you want, big guy?"

Thaddeus opened his mouth and said, "Food. Food.

Food."

Doreen bolted to her feet, looked at the animals, and said, "You can't be hungry again."

Yet, with guilt ripping through her, she fed them all over again. Goliath sauntered over, took a few bites, and lay down in front of his food bowl, as if in disgust. On the other hand, Mugs had no problem devouring his bowl of food. He wandered over toward Goliath and sniffed, then he lay down but shoved Goliath back a little bit. The cat reached out and swiped his paw across Mugs's head. But then Goliath got up and walked away. Mugs then devoured Goliath's lunch too. Doreen stared at him. "Mugs! Since when do you eat cat food?"

Mack chuckled. "Lots of dogs have appetite-control issues. In this case, I think it's just jealousy."

"Oh, for heaven's sake," she said as she pulled away the rest of Goliath's lunch, then set the bowl on the counter so Mugs couldn't inhale any more. She washed her hands, only to turn around and see Thaddeus working away on Goliath's food. "No, wait," she cried out and raced to Thaddeus. She snagged the cat's bowl and glared at Thaddeus. "That's not bird food."

"It's bird food," he said. "It's bird food." And he hopped up on her arm and started pecking away at the bowl.

Stunned, Doreen looked at Mack, who shrugged and said, "In the wild, birds will eat all kinds of things, including cat food and dog food. So I doubt it will hurt him. What kind is it?"

She looked at the label on the can still on the counter and said, "Fish."

"Well, there you go. I'm sure Thaddeus won't be hurt from having a little fish."

"But it's Goliath's food," she said. "How will I keep track of who's eating what and making sure they're getting enough if they eat everybody else's food?"

"Don't worry about it right now," Mack said gently. "You've been distracted. What are the chances you didn't feed them this morning?"

She cast her mind back and then shrugged. "I have no clue. If I did, it would explain why Goliath isn't interested." She walked to where she kept a bowl of birdseed for Thaddeus, and it was empty. She frowned and shrugged. "I honestly don't know." But she moved Thaddeus to the table and put the rest of the cat food in a sealed baggie and into the fridge. She closed the fridge with a *thunk*.

"What about you?" Mack asked. "Did you eat?"

"I got up late, so I didn't eat much," she confessed. "And it is lunchtime. Maybe a sandwich." She pulled out the fixings for a sandwich, and then stopped and looked at Mack suspiciously. "Are you hungry?"

He gave her a smile. "So, does that mean I'm invited to have a sandwich with you, or does that mean you think I'm staying long enough so I can mooch a sandwich off you?"

Instantly, she felt guilty. "There's enough for two sandwiches," she said, grandly trying to put her own suspicions behind her. "And, yes, I do owe you a sandwich."

"You don't owe me anything," Mack said, reaching into the fridge and finding a tomato and lettuce, rooting around for anything else, grabbing two plates, then walking to the table, pulling out four slices of bread. "But, yes, thank you. I'll have a sandwich. When I haven't had any sleep, I need more food to keep going."

Doreen felt bad. "I'm sorry. You're right. It's been a pretty rough day all-around."

"That it has," Mack said. He sat down and proceeded to make himself a sandwich. She worked alongside him and made herself one too. He went easy on the meat but heavy on the vegetables. She watched in fascination as he added layers to his sandwich. He put pickles on first; then he put peppers, tomatoes, onions, lettuce, and she just stared when he went to pick it up.

"How can you even get your mouth around that?"

He shot her a look and said, "Easy." And he took a big bite. Hers was about half that tall. She sat beside him and ate hers too.

"Are you sure it was Steve in his house fire?" she asked out of the blue.

He turned to her and said, "That's up to the coroner to decide."

She nodded. "Right. I guess that makes sense." As she kept eating, her mind was busy with the various cases. "If everybody's dead, I guess the cases get closed?"

"If we have enough proof and evidence that we know who and what was behind it all, and everybody involved is deceased, then, yes, it would close with notes to that effect."

She nodded. "Well, that would be nice." Then she brightened. "We can get on the Bob Small case."

He munched his sandwich, but she could feel his growing angry vibes.

She sighed, took another bite, swallowed, and then added, "Or maybe not."

He sagged in his chair, popped the last bite of his sandwich in his mouth, and said, "Definitely not."

And then he hopped up and poured two cups of coffee. He gave her one as she finished her sandwich. "As soon as I've had this, I'm gone."

She nodded. "Makes sense to me."

So they sat outside, both tired but happy they were where they needed to be in life. Finally, Mack finished his cup and left. Doreen watched him leave almost sadly. But, in his case, he was like a boomerang. The more he left, the more he came back.

And she was starting to realize just what a darn good thing that was.

# Chapter 32

*Friday Afternoon …*

DOREEN STRAIGHTENED UP from her hoeing. Her work in Millicent's garden was going well. It was a gray overcast day, and, with any luck, she'd be done in no time. Which was a good thing, considering the threat of rain later. She could have come yesterday, but she'd gotten into the rhythm of Fridays so hadn't wanted to change it. Thursday had passed in a blur of her own gardening and research and wondering, plus her first attempt at making spaghetti herself, then back to her gardening to keep her busy while she waited for more answers.

So far, there weren't any.

She smiled at Millicent, who came out with a piece of zucchini bread and a cup of tea.

"How are you this afternoon?" Doreen asked.

"I'm fine," Millicent said. "I wasn't sure if I would see you or not today."

"True enough," Doreen said cheerfully. "But I'm trying to maintain a Friday schedule, though it might go off the rails once in a while. Of course, I never slow down. And that's all good. At this rate, we're starting to get this place tuned up nicely."

"Are you okay to maybe cut back the lawn edge in that garden bed a bit?" Millicent's tone sounded anxious, as if worrying that Doreen wasn't prepared to do this.

Doreen looked at her and said, "Of course. Do you have a grass edger?"

Millicent nodded. "I think it is in the shed." She slowly made her way down the steps, even against Doreen's protests, and headed to the shed, then brought out an edger.

"How far back do you want me to expose?" Doreen asked. Together they sorted out a two-inch line, and Doreen went along and cut and broke up the sod so the garden bed and the sod wouldn't encroach on each other. "It's a nice and easy way to keep it clean, isn't it?"

By the time she got all the way to the rear fence and around the back to come down on the other side, she could feel her arms aching. She took a break, went back, and removed all the pieces she had cut. Then she carried them to the compost pile. As soon as she was done, she went back and raked the garden edge.

"That looks fantastic," Millicent said warmly.

"It makes a big difference, doesn't it?" Doreen returned the grass edger to the shed. As she walked toward Millicent, she said, "And just in the nick of time too." Her hours were up, so, with a wave, she collected her critters and headed back to the creek.

She was just hot and tired enough that, by the time she made it to her place, she stayed at the creek and stood barefoot in the cool water. The water had risen, so several more rocks were underwater. She stared in amazement, then bent down and grabbed several handfuls of cold water and splashed her face. After that, she sat on one of the few rocks in the middle that was still dry.

"It's been a good day," she said to the animals.

Mugs walked into the center of the creek to find himself swimming. She called him back to shore.

"Well, that's a surprise," she said. "I hadn't thought it was that deep."

Cautiously he took a few more steps forward, and it appeared to be just over his height, so he started to float. It went down fairly steep on one edge. Doreen realized the current was getting stronger. She could imagine it would be quite something by the time the river runoffs came through. With Mugs now thoroughly cooled off, and Thaddeus sitting on a rock enjoying the cool breeze, she plunked her butt down beside the bird and let her body relax. Her life was so much different here, so free compared to what it used to be. Thaddeus hopped onto her shoulder and gently cuddled against her neck. "Not only is it so much freer," she whispered to him, "but it's also a whole lot more loving."

He rubbed his head against her and said, "Thaddeus loves Doreen. Thaddeus loves Doreen."

Overwhelmed with joy by hearing those words and wondering how long it had been since she'd heard anybody say they loved her, she held him close for a long moment, feeling tears prickle in the corner of her eyes. Not to be outdone, Mugs came around in front of her and jumped up so his front paws were on the rock between her legs. She smiled and gave the hairy wet mass a cuddle. "We will never get you dry," she said. "I think that means we'll lie out in the grass and just rest this afternoon."

But then she looked at her own garden, and guilt went through her. "Or not," she said with a heavy sigh. It was a great day for gardening, and she wasn't terribly tired after her short rest, so maybe she could do a little bit more. She got up and walked back to the porch, found her gloves where she'd left them alongside her digging fork and dug up the next couple feet of weeds with the animals lying around beside her.

She worked happily until she heard someone call out.

She yelled, "I'm out back," but there was no answer.

She waited, thinking surely it must have been Mack, although it was pretty early for him. She walked back in the kitchen door and through to the living room, but she found no sign of anybody. Frowning, she peered out the front door, but again she saw nothing. However, a bunch of people out front were talking to one of her neighbors. Thankfully none of them were journalists. They all seemed to talk excitedly about plans, then piled into vehicles and left.

Surprised, but figuring it must have been noise from that group or one of the other neighbors—since they did make noise occasionally—and studying both of her front doors, she shrugged and headed back outside. She was almost done with what she'd planned to do in her backyard for the day, but not quite. She returned to her garden; the animals were once again in tow, collapsing on the lawn around her. She finished up along one bed, finding it full of painted daisies, black-eyed Susans, and echinacea. Basically, all the same look of a daisy flower but in yellow, pink, purple, and white. It would be stunning.

Except … they would flower at different times. The white daisies would open soon. Well, not very soon. She studied the buds and saw they were still quite tight. But they were forming. So, maybe within a month.

She continued to work, forcing herself to go past her

two-hour time allotment and having a mental argument with herself as to when she should quit. Then finally, she'd had enough. Thirsty and tired, she stepped back and saw she was halfway done with the one long bed to the house.

She really liked the idea of what Millicent had done with her garden and the edger. Doreen wasn't sure she had one of those though, but it was a good idea. And, if she could ever get stepping stones, she would put them down in a gravel base to make a simple path to the creek. Inspired by the design and, with ideas flowing through her, she walked back into the kitchen and poured herself a big glass of water. Then she sat down with her notepad and designing a curved path around the weeping maple that needed some TLC and continued drawing with the path down toward the creek.

She had some big grassy spots that needed aerating and fertilizing, and she didn't even know if a lawn mower was to be had around this place. The grass was getting long in spots, just not in enough spots to be worth mowing. She laughed. "I could probably take scissors to the long blades of weeds."

By the time she was done, she straightened, rotated her neck, and rose to put on a cup of tea. She should take her cup and sit out front. Maybe she could come up with some ideas for the front yard too. When the teakettle boiled, she got herself a cup and headed to the front door, opening it, and froze.

She grabbed her phone and called Mack.

"What's the matter?" he said, his voice distracted.

"I need you, and I need you now," she snapped. And she hung up.

She lifted her nose and smelled again. There was no doubt about it. It was gasoline. She took a long moment to assess what would burn in the front and what wouldn't burn and what she could do about it. Water on gasoline she didn't think was a good idea. And then she remembered dirt. That would be the best solution and wouldn't harm the grass. Maybe that was the only thing that would help. Oh, why didn't she have a pile of topsoil to use? But Richard had a small pile on the side of his garage. She ran into her garage and grabbed the wheelbarrow and a shovel and raced to Richard's property. She shoveled the wheelbarrow full then struggled to push it to her property and up the driveway. Richard didn't appear to notice her actions as he wasn't yelling at her. By the time she pushed the wheelbarrow to where it was needed, she was sniffing the air, looking for the smell. When she found it, she covered up the line of liquid all around the house with dirt.

When Mack drove up twenty minutes later, he asked, "Now what are you up to? Do you really think some kind of witch's hex will stop the bad guys from getting at you?"

She gave him a hard look. "Gasoline."

The smile wore off his face. He sniffed and nodded. He called the fire marshal and somebody else. Doreen didn't know who or what. Her body involuntarily shook as she realized how close this had been. So why was the house not on fire? Why hadn't someone lit the fuel?

"Did you see anyone?" Mack asked.

She shook her head wildly. "I thought I heard somebody call out to me about an hour ago, and I thought it was you, honestly. I came to the front door and saw a group of people at a neighbor's place, and they were laughing, making plans, then all took off. I didn't see anyone else."

"When did you notice the gasoline?"

"Not very long ago. I was gardening in the back. I came in, got water, and I planned to sit with a cup of tea in the front to see if I got any garden ideas. That's when I smelled the gas fumes. That's when I called you too. Then I ran over to my neighbor's and grabbed the dirt from his pile. I owe him now." She pointed in her neighbor's direction only to see Richard standing there in the front door, his gaze looking at her wheelbarrow and pile of dirt with a big dent in the side.

Richard roared, "Did you just steal that?"

"I did," she said. "And you're welcome."

Confusion rippled across his features. He obviously didn't understand.

"Did you see anyone here in the last hour?" Mack called over to Richard.

He lifted a hand to cup around his ear; then, as if finally processing Mack's words, Richard shrugged. "I did see somebody, but I didn't think anything of it. She's got so many people around here all the time. You should chase them off for ruining the peace and quiet around here."

Mack ignored that part. "Did he have a gas can?"

Richard looked at them, and then he looked at the dirt and the line she had poured all around the property. She could see the details filtering into his system. He nodded slowly. "He had something, but I didn't know that it was a gas can. It was a big jug."

"Would you recognize who it was?"

He stared at Mack and then over at Doreen. "Did somebody just try to burn down your house?"

"I don't know if they planned to or not, but I presume so," she said slowly. "They didn't light a match. That's the part I don't get."

"Second thoughts?" Richard asked.

She shook her head. "I don't know. Likely interrupted

and planning to come back later to finish the job." And because she didn't know, it really worried her. Within minutes, more vehicles pulled up.

Richard shot her an ugly look and said, "See what I mean? She's always got people here." He bolted inside his door and slammed it hard.

The fire marshal hopped out of his vehicle, came over, and shook Mack's hand but then caught a whiff of the gasoline. His sharp gaze noted the dirt ring around the house and let out a long, slow whistle. He turned to Doreen and said, "Somebody really hates you."

She crossed her arms over her chest. "And some people have good reason to hate me," she said calmly. "With my assistance, they'll go to jail for the rest of their lives."

The fire marshal looked at her, saw Mugs and Goliath at her feet and Thaddeus on the crook of her neck, and said, "You're the bone lady."

She nodded. "Yes, and it's no coincidence we're current-ly involved in a case that involves arson."

He nodded. "Let me take a look." He went inside, while outside his team wrapped around the property, looking. When he came back, he said, "This is standard fuel-grade gasoline. It's only on the outside of the house. It's a potential circle of fire, but you have thoroughly covered it with dirt." Then he took out a lighter and showed her that nothing would burn. She could feel some of her stress inside abating.

"But we don't know that he's finished," she said. "Or if he's done something else."

"I would say he's definitely not done," the fire marshal said as he looked at her. "There was no reason for him to not toss a match except for the fact it's broad daylight, and chances are he would have been caught before too much damage was done."

"Or somebody interrupted him," Mack said. He looked down at Mugs and said, "How was Mugs when you were checking out the front?"

"He didn't come with me," she said. "He was barking in the back."

"Ah …"

Doreen froze and looked at him. "What?" she asked.

"It's quite possible the intruder thought you weren't home," Mack said. "And when he realized the dog was out back, and you had come into the front of the house, after thinking you heard something out front, he found out you *were* home. He might have also taken the opportunity to pour more gasoline while you were in the backyard again."

"That would mean he wasn't planning to kill me first, then to burn my body," she said slowly. "I do prefer that version."

"Or at least didn't want to kill you in broad daylight where he might get caught," the fire marshal added. He looked at Mack and said, "I'll write this up, but this will be something you guys need to keep an eye on. And find the firebug as soon as possible."

Mack nodded. "You mean, before he tries this again."

The fire marshal barely hid a chuckle as he nodded. "Exactly."

He left, and there was Arnold, staring at her with a grim look in his eye.

"I didn't see anybody," she said, trying to be helpful. "I did hear a sound, as if somebody was calling out to see if I was home though."

"That's the only good thing about this," Arnold said. "The fact of the matter is, if he didn't try to kill you today, chances are he wasn't looking to kill but just to burn down your property."

She reached up and rubbed her temple. "It doesn't make any sense."

"Nothing has to make sense," Mack said. "Come on. Let's get you back inside the house."

She went back in and then stopped and said, "I have to return the rest of this dirt to my neighbor."

"Leave it," he said. "We'll take pictures."

Her shoulders sagged, and she nodded, calling Mugs and Goliath in with her. Then she turned to Mack and asked, "Are you coming in too?"

"I have to talk to the guys first."

She nodded and went in to put on coffee. If there was one thing she was sure of, Mack wouldn't say no to a cup of coffee. And, right now, she really needed the caffeine. She also didn't want Mack to leave. The fire marshal had checked to make sure no gasoline was anywhere in the house, so that made her feel better. But … not good enough. With the coffee dripping, she walked over to her little office alcove, picked up the stack she had meant to take to Rosemoor—the ones Nan had asked her to scan—and walked back out front.

"I need to get away for a few moments," she said. "I'll deliver this to Nan."

Mack nodded. "I'll be here when you come back, unless I get called away."

"Right," she said, and she rushed off. On the way, she called Nan, but there was no answer. She groaned. When she got to Nan's patio, Nan really wasn't there. Doreen frowned, then shrugged it off. Nan had a better social life than Doreen did. She wrote a note on the envelope and left it on Nan's outdoor patio table. It was safe from the elements there.

Still, it was disappointing. She needed a hug right now. Slowly and out of sorts, she walked back alongside the creek. At her property, she stopped and stared at the house, wondering what she was supposed to do about this new element. She walked back inside and took a look outside to see two cops still talking out front but nobody else. She groaned, sat down at the kitchen table, and said, "And now what?"

"And now," a man said behind her, "now you get to commit suicide and burn."

She froze, turned ever-so-slightly, and smiled. "So I was right," she crowed.

Steve stared at her. "You were right about what?"

She looked at the gun in his hand and waved it off. "Nobody will believe I committed suicide with a gun," she said with a shake of her head. "You really don't research your victims first, do you?"

# Chapter 33

*Friday Afternoon …*

STEVE FROWNED. "WHAT are you talking about?"

"First off, I'd never commit suicide. Period. Nobody here will believe that. And the gasoline has been covered in dirt now. It won't burn."

He shrugged. "I can come back with more."

"Sure you could. It would break your pattern though."

He stared at Doreen, anger growing on his face. "What difference does it make?"

"It's a pattern. And patterns matter to serial arsonists—and serial killers. And …" And that's when she realized what he had planned for her. "You were planning to repeat your pattern with me. Pour gasoline outside, come inside, and help me to commit 'suicide,' then light my body on fire, like the gang was supposed to do in the first place. Then you planned to go outside and light up the gasoline, waiting there to keep any rescuers outside of the house while I burn to nothing, leaving zero left forensically for them to understand what happened. Particularly given that this old house will go up like a matchstick."

He nodded slowly. "You're not so stupid after all."

"No," she said cheerfully, feeling an exuberance she had no business feeling. "I'm not stupid at all. And I was right."

"What are you talking about?" he asked, glaring at her.

"I already asked Mack if they had proven it wasn't you in that fire yesterday. And told him to check for your money laundering schemes and to study your bank accounts against the checks you wrote those women."

He stared at her in shock.

She nodded. "No way you would have committed suicide in that house. And the only way to get out of town and have all of this go away was to make sure you were dead. At least *appeared* to be dead. That way anyone from the Devil Riders' gang who might still be gunning for you would give up. Too bad you aren't really dead. It would be fitting if you'd died alongside those poor women you killed. And all for what? Greed? Secrecy? Because they were part of the other gang?"

The shocked look on his face was priceless. "How did you know about them?" he asked in a hoarse whisper. "How did you know about any of it?"

"By knowing who you were on the inside," she said gently. "You'd never let them go. Any one of those women could have gone to the cops, and you'd have all gone down. And you'd be caught for money laundering for the gang and they, in turn, would have taken you out for getting caught."

"And they would have," he stated categorically. "You couldn't trust them. The gang or the women. And, if that was the case, no way could they be allowed to cash those checks. So I handed out checks that any bank employee, if worth their salt, would reject. I misspelled the women's name each time, so, when showing ID at any bank, their legal names would not match up with the check I gave them.

You'd be surprised how people miss that and zoom in right for the amount instead. Then they'd have to contact me for replacement checks that they could then cash. I was renovating at the time, so I took them all out within the same day and used the heavy equipment on the place to bury them deep." He shook his head. "I still don't understand how you figured that out."

"Well, I didn't know for sure about the location of the bodies but thanks for the clarification. Now they can be exhumed and buried properly and allow their families some closure. And I suppose you shot them with the same gun that was found in my neighbor's yard, huh? Why get a new weapon when that one worked so well? And did you plan to shoot me when you came through my yard with it that night Penny was with you? You must have really loved her to try and kill me like that." She smiled up at him. "Too bad you didn't just leave town. You might have been able to stay dead."

"Well, appearing dead is one thing, but I also needed to make sure one nasty busybody who was ruining my life was dead too," he cried, cocking the gun in his hand. "I didn't stand a chance back then and look at all the damage you've caused since then…"

"I get that," she said gently. "I really do. But the fact of the matter is, you still won't get away with it."

"And why is that?" he asked with a snort.

She smiled and said, "Because of this." And just then Goliath, who'd been creeping up behind him, jumped as high as he could and caught hold of Steve midspine. Knowing the gun was leveled at her, she dove for the ground as it went off. With gunfire inside, she knew the cops outside would race toward her.

Not to be outdone, Thaddeus, who'd been sitting on the kitchen table, flew up to Steve's gun hand and pecked away on it. Steve was still screaming and trying to shake off the cat, stumbling around, when Mugs caught him with a bite behind the knees. He went down hard on his butt. Doreen picked up the cast-iron frying pan she swore she would use one day. It took two hands to lift it, and, just as she went to swing it at his head, he reached up an arm in a defensive move, and the skillet came down hard on his elbow.

*Crack …*

He roared in agony as the front door burst open. Mack and the cops ran in.

The gun skittered across the kitchen floor, and Mack stared at her in shock.

She stepped back. "Look at this. This cast-iron skillet really does come in handy," she said admiringly as she placed it gently on the kitchen table. "But you know something, Mack? I think I need one about half that size."

He glared at her, while Steve, still on the floor, screamed, "She's crazy. She's absolutely crazy!"

At that, Goliath sauntered past again and swiped Steve hard across his cheek. Steve roared as his cheek erupted in bleeding scratches. And Mugs, obviously just as offended, took one look at Steve's ankle stretched out in front of him and bit down hard.

Steve screamed again, then yelled, "Get them off me! Get them off me!"

Mack laughed, but he helped Mugs calm down enough so he would release his jaw. Then Mack turned to Doreen. "Get them away from here."

She gave him a look. "Why? They're just defending my honor," she snapped.

He rolled his eyes and said, "I don't think it's necessary any longer. Steve's done, and he's down. You're good."

She smiled and called Mugs and Goliath to her. Thaddeus too. "Come on, big guy," she crooned. "I'm safe now. Come on. Calm down."

He walked over, clucking and, obviously upset at what had happened, half flew and half jumped on Mugs's back. With the four of them gathered together, Doreen crouched down and put an arm around them. She sat here and watched as Mack helped Steve to his feet.

He stood, shaky but upright, hugging his injured arm against his chest.

"See? I was right," she told Mack. "It definitely wasn't Steve in that fire."

Mack groaned. "I got it," he said. "But you might want to consider that we'd like to sort some things out on our own."

Arnold, however, didn't have a problem with her solving the case. He reached out to give her a high five. "You know those animals need a commendation for the work they do," he said.

She chuckled. "Isn't that the truth? At least now you have more cold cases solved."

Arnold looked at her then, his face paling. "What?"

"Steve was involved in covering up four murders of gang members about twenty-two years ago," she said. "Mack has the confession already from a woman involved in all four of them. Her husband was in the Devil Riders' gang and was murdered by the rival gang. So the Devil Riders took out four members of the rival gang in retaliation."

Arnold stared at her, reaching up to scratch his head. Then he shook his head and muttered on his way out about too much work. Mack looked at Doreen, sighed.

"I'm fine," she muttered. "Still, you're welcome."

He chuckled, snagged her up, and gave her a big hug. "Now will you sleep tonight?"

She nodded. "I'll sleep like a baby. Another job well done."

# Epilogue

***Friday late afternoon …***

"ALL YOU NEED to do now," Mack said, "is stay out of trouble."

Doreen shrugged. "How much trouble can I get in? I've been gardening all day, and I'm coming up to the big hydrangea bush. There's no trouble I can get into with that."

He just looked at her. "Hydrangeas?"

She shrugged. "Those big flowering plants. I promise I'll spend tomorrow working in my garden."

He stared at her in doubt.

She chuckled. "Of course, I can't guarantee what I might find."

"You don't get to find anything," he said, a warning in his tone.

"Well, why not? There was a gun in the gardenias. Maybe I'll find …" She stopped, pondered for a moment. "How about I find handcuffs in the hydrangeas?" she announced triumphantly.

"How about you don't? How about you just stop trying to find anything?" And, with that, he turned and stormed out.

Mutinously, she watched him walk out the front door. She trailed behind him, her gaze falling on the wheelbarrow with the little bit of dirt left. She still had to return the last of it to her neighbor.

She picked in the handles to the wheelbarrow and pushed it over to his house. There she rapped on the door. When he opened it, glaring at her suspiciously, she said, "I just brought this back. I promise to get you some more for the bit I used."

He shook his head. "Don't bother. That's all extra anyway. It's there because I'm supposed to spread it in the front garden but haven't gotten around to it."

She nodded and said, "Well, thank you for the dirt I used."

And she lifted it from her wheelbarrow and put it up at the corner of the garage. As she turned the wheelbarrow around, she looked at the hydrangeas in his garden and said, "This garden is doing really well. And that heather is gorgeous. The hydrangea is looking lovely too."

"The hydrangea is nice. It's the blue-flowering variety."

As she studied the bush, she wondered out loud, "I'm surprised that bush is so small though."

He shrugged. "It's been small since forever. I don't know why. Probably no room up against the house."

She wondered. "May I take a look?"

He stared at her suspiciously. "What could you possibly look at?"

But she eyed something flashing in the light. Only it wasn't in the hydrangeas, but rather in the blooming heather in front of the bigger bush.

"Who knows? Something could be restricting the bush's root system." At least that gave her an excuse to get in the garden bed.

She crouched at the edge of the hydrangeas to where the heather had tangled up in something metallic.

Almost immediately she identified the item. She gasped, shocked, and then she laughed. Very carefully she scooped away the leaves and the mulch that had piled up over the years.

And sure enough, she found a set of handcuffs, one of which was caught around the plant.

She sat back and howled with laughter. It wasn't handcuffs in the hydrangeas. Instead, it was handcuffs in the heather …

Who'd have guessed?

Even better that they were torn and very much worse-for-wear pink satin handcuffs. … She snickered.

Wait until she told Mack …

This concludes Book 7 of Lovely Lethal Gardens: Gun in the Gardenias.

Read about Handcuffs in the Heather: Lovely Lethal Gardens, Book 8

# Lovely Lethal Gardens: Handcuffs in the Heather (Book #8)

**A new cozy mystery series from USA Today best-selling author Dale Mayer. Follow gardener and amateur sleuth Doreen Montgomery—and her amusing and mostly lovable cat, dog, and parrot—as they catch murderers and solve crimes in lovely Kelowna, British Columbia.**

*Riches to rags. … Everything is under control, … until it isn't. And Doreen's in the middle of it!*

The four boxes of files Doreen inherited from journalist Bridgeman Solomon have already helped her solve one crime, and Doreen hopes they'll continue to assist her as she sticks her nose into future cases. But, when she stumbles over a pair of pink satin handcuffs in her standoffish neighbor Richard de Genaro's heather patch, it's hard to believe that those reporter's files could have anything useful to offer regarding that.

Doreen takes a look though, and soon she's headed down a merry trail of prostitution, embezzlement, and, of course, murder. But the minute the files suggest a connection to Doreen's specialty, a cold case, her beau and partner in crime, Corporal Mack Moreau, starts breathing down her neck.

"

With her trusty animals leading the way, Doreen sets out to find the connection between the reputable banker who died in an unsolved hit-and-run and the prostitute who owned the pink satin handcuffs. As Doreen puts it all together, even she is surprised at the outcome of her latest investigation.

Book 8 is available now!
To find out more visit Dale Mayer's website.
https://geni.us/DMHandcuffsUniversal

# Author's Note

Thank you for reading Gun in the Gardenias: Lovely Lethal Gardens, Book 7! If you enjoyed the book, please take a moment and leave a short review.

Dear reader,

I love to hear from readers, and you can contact me at my website: www.dalemayer.com or at my Facebook author page. To be informed of new releases and special offers, sign up for my newsletter or follow me on BookBub. And if you are interested in joining Dale Mayer's Reader Group, here is the Facebook sign up page.
http://geni.us/DaleMayerFBGroup

Cheers,
Dale Mayer

# About the Author

Dale Mayer is a *USA Today* best-selling author, best known for her SEALs military romances, her Psychic Visions series, and her Lovely Lethal Garden cozy series. Her contemporary romances are raw and full of passion and emotion (Broken But … Mending, Hathaway House series). Her thrillers will keep you guessing (Kate Morgan, By Death series), and her romantic comedies will keep you giggling (*It's a Dog's Life*, a stand-alone novella; and the Broken Protocols series, starring Charming Marvin, the cat).

Dale honors the stories that come to her—and some of them are crazy, break all the rules and cross multiple genres!

To go with her fiction, she also writes nonfiction in many different fields, with books available on résumé writing, companion gardening, and the US mortgage system. All her books are available in print and ebook format.

## Connect with Dale Mayer Online

*Dale's Website – www.dalemayer.com*
*Twitter – @DaleMayer*
*Facebook Page – geni.us/DaleMayerFBFanPage*
*Facebook Group – geni.us/DaleMayerFBGroup*
*BookBub – geni.us/DaleMayerBookbub*
*Instagram – geni.us/DaleMayerInstagram*
*Goodreads – geni.us/DaleMayerGoodreads*
*Newsletter – geni.us/DaleNews*

# Also by Dale Mayer

## Published Adult Books:

### Hathaway House
Aaron, Book 1
Brock, Book 2
Cole, Book 3
Denton, Book 4
Elliot, Book 5
Finn, Book 6

### The K9 Files
Ethan, Book 1
Pierce, Book 2
Zane, Book 3
Blaze, Book 4
Lucas, Book 5
Parker, Book 6
Carter, Book 7

### Lovely Lethal Gardens
Arsenic in the Azaleas, Book 1
Bones in the Begonias, Book 2
Corpse in the Carnations, Book 3
Daggers in the Dahlias, Book 4
Evidence in the Echinacea, Book 5
Footprints in the Ferns, Book 6

Gun in the Gardenias, Book 7
Handcuffs in the Heather, Book 8

## Psychic Vision Series
Tuesday's Child
Hide 'n Go Seek
Maddy's Floor
Garden of Sorrow
Knock Knock…
Rare Find
Eyes to the Soul
Now You See Her
Shattered
Into the Abyss
Seeds of Malice
Eye of the Falcon
Itsy-Bitsy Spider
Unmasked
Deep Beneath
From the Ashes
Psychic Visions Books 1–3
Psychic Visions Books 4–6
Psychic Visions Books 7–9

## By Death Series
Touched by Death
Haunted by Death
Chilled by Death
By Death Books 1–3

## Broken Protocols – Romantic Comedy Series
Cat's Meow

Cat's Pajamas
Cat's Cradle
Cat's Claus
Broken Protocols 1-4

## Broken and... Mending

Skin
Scars
Scales (of Justice)
Broken but... Mending 1-3

## Glory

Genesis
Tori
Celeste
Glory Trilogy

## Biker Blues

Morgan: Biker Blues, Volume 1
Cash: Biker Blues, Volume 2

## SEALs of Honor

Mason: SEALs of Honor, Book 1
Hawk: SEALs of Honor, Book 2
Dane: SEALs of Honor, Book 3
Swede: SEALs of Honor, Book 4
Shadow: SEALs of Honor, Book 5
Cooper: SEALs of Honor, Book 6
Markus: SEALs of Honor, Book 7
Evan: SEALs of Honor, Book 8
Mason's Wish: SEALs of Honor, Book 9
Chase: SEALs of Honor, Book 10
Brett: SEALs of Honor, Book 11

Devlin: SEALs of Honor, Book 12
Easton: SEALs of Honor, Book 13
Ryder: SEALs of Honor, Book 14
Macklin: SEALs of Honor, Book 15
Corey: SEALs of Honor, Book 16
Warrick: SEALs of Honor, Book 17
Tanner: SEALs of Honor, Book 18
Jackson: SEALs of Honor, Book 19
Kanen: SEALs of Honor, Book 20
Nelson: SEALs of Honor, Book 21
Taylor: SEALs of Honor, Book 22
SEALs of Honor, Books 1–3
SEALs of Honor, Books 4–6
SEALs of Honor, Books 7–10
SEALs of Honor, Books 11–13
SEALs of Honor, Books 14–16
SEALs of Honor, Books 17–19

## Heroes for Hire

Levi's Legend: Heroes for Hire, Book 1
Stone's Surrender: Heroes for Hire, Book 2
Merk's Mistake: Heroes for Hire, Book 3
Rhodes's Reward: Heroes for Hire, Book 4
Flynn's Firecracker: Heroes for Hire, Book 5
Logan's Light: Heroes for Hire, Book 6
Harrison's Heart: Heroes for Hire, Book 7
Saul's Sweetheart: Heroes for Hire, Book 8
Dakota's Delight: Heroes for Hire, Book 9
Michael's Mercy (Part of Sleeper SEAL Series)
Tyson's Treasure: Heroes for Hire, Book 10
Jace's Jewel: Heroes for Hire, Book 11
Rory's Rose: Heroes for Hire, Book 12

## Standalone Novellas

It's a Dog's Life
Riana's Revenge
Second Chances

# Published Young Adult Books:

## Family Blood Ties Series

Vampire in Denial
Vampire in Distress
Vampire in Design
Vampire in Deceit
Vampire in Defiance
Vampire in Conflict
Vampire in Chaos
Vampire in Crisis
Vampire in Control
Vampire in Charge
Family Blood Ties Set 1–3
Family Blood Ties Set 1–5
Family Blood Ties Set 4–6
Family Blood Ties Set 7–9
Sian's Solution, A Family Blood Ties Series Prequel
      Novelette

## Design series

Dangerous Designs
Deadly Designs
Darkest Designs
Design Series Trilogy

**Standalone**

In Cassie's Corner

Gem Stone (a Gemma Stone Mystery)

Time Thieves

# Published Non-Fiction Books:

**Career Essentials**

Career Essentials: The Résumé

Career Essentials: The Cover Letter

Career Essentials: The Interview

Career Essentials: 3 in 1